Sour Grapes

Middle East Literature in Translation
Michael Beard and Adnan Haydar, *Series Editors*

Select Titles in Middle East Literature and Translation

Animals in Our Days: A Book of Stories
Mohamed Makhzangi; Chip Rossetti, trans.

The Heart of Lebanon
Ameen Rihani; Roger Allen, trans.

Hot Maroc: A Novel
Yassin Adnan; Alexander E. Elinson, trans.

Island of Bewilderment: A Novel of Modern Iran
Simin Daneshvar; Patricia J. Higgins
and Pouneh Shabani-Jadidi, trans.

Packaged Lives: Ten Stories and a Novella
Haifa Zangana; Wen-chin Ouyang, trans.

Solitaire: A Novel
Hassouna Mosbahi; William Maynard Hutchins, trans.

Sons of the People: The Mamluk Trilogy
Reem Bassiouney; Roger Allen, trans.

Waiting for the Past: A Novel
Hadiya Hussein; Barbara Romaine, trans.

For a full list of titles in this series,
visit https://press.syr.edu/supressbook-series
/middle-east-literature-in-translation.

Sour Grapes

Zakaria Tamer

Translated from the Arabic by
Alessandro Columbu
and Mireia Costa Capallera

Introduction by
Nader K. Uthman

Syracuse University Press

Originally published in Arabic as الحصرم (*al-Ḥiṣrim*)
(London: Riad El-Rayyes Book).

First Edition 2023

23 24 25 26 27 28   6 5 4 3 2 1

∞ The paper used in this publication meets the minimum requirements
of the American National Standard for Information Sciences—Permanence
of Paper for Printed Library Materials, ANSI Z39.48-1992.

For a listing of books published and distributed by Syracuse University Press,
visit https://press.syr.edu.

ISBN: 978-0-8156-1154-7 (paperback)   978-0-8156-5584-8 (e-book)

Library of Congress Control Number: 2023933978

Manufactured in the United States of America

*He said, "O my son, do not
relate your vision to your brothers"*

The Noble Qur'an, Surah Yusuf

Contents

Introduction

Among his wide-ranging oeuvre of children's stories, satirical articles, literary criticism and for some years, a regular column in *Al-Quds Al-Arabi*, Zakariyya Tamer (b. 1931) is best known for his short story collections, especially the *very* short story (al-qissa al-qasira jiddan). These may range from a few lines or several paragraphs to a few pages, and yet these beguilingly simple glimpses linger with the reader, due to Tamer's lyrical style, surprising plot twists, and frank themes. *Sour Grapes* explodes with knifings, rapes, and gang attacks, while Tamer eagerly lances sacred cows and social niceties with acid barbs and an arch style. One of the chief devices he puts to use in his stories is peripety, "the sudden reversal of a character's circumstances and fortunes, usually involving the downfall of a protagonist in a tragedy. . . ."[1] As such, a rapist is reduced to a squealing victim, or

---

1. Chris Baldick, "peripeteia," in *The Oxford Dictionary of Literary Term*s (Oxford University Press); *Oxford Reference*, accessed 10 July 2022, https://www-oxfordreference-com.ezp

sweethearts who, after much wooing and falling in love, suddenly find each other repugnant, obliterating their initial attraction. Tamer's style is cultured and yet not overly proper, at times reverting to informal, spoken Arabic. The repetition of phrases generates rhythmic passages, while drawing on a dizzying array of fantastic images culled from medieval and modern literature, contemporary life, history, and folklore. As in his other collections, *Sour Grapes* features characters familiar from folktales the world over: peasants and potentates, spinsters and recluses, soldiers and officials, schemers, dupes, and shrill crones. *Sour Grapes* is both familiar and fantastic: speaking cats, tree branches that show envy, corpses that speak, and body parts that commune with the person to whom they're attached. In the story "The Green Bird," Abu Hayyan Al-Tawhidi, the tenth-century scholar, effortlessly transforms into a lamb, a cat, a wolf, "and eventually into a green-feathered bird."

Tamer confounds our expectations of an ordered society based on collective morality, as well as the notion of justice itself, in order to advance his brand of social critique. Ultimately, it is our public adherence to dubious mores that is among his most cherished targets. In the story titled "The Disgraced" (al-muftadih), a single character, Ghalib al-Hallas, is

-prod1.hul.harvard.edu/view/10.1093/acref/9780199208272
.001.0001/acref-9780199208272-e-862.

barely revealed to the reader after the introductory line, "Ghalib al-Hallas is a disgraced man." What follows is a laundry list of ghastly, rebarbative, and at times comedic descriptions of the offenses of his family: a father who only desired women who reeked of onion and garlic, a sister whose insanity was "contagious," a brother who sold dog meat as lamb, as well a wife and son who debase themselves for sex. Born a bastard, whose many riches were illegally procured, al-Hallas paid no heed to the "scandals" around him and "kept walking amongst people on a red carpet" as he grew richer through fraud. His and his family's misdeeds invite us to gape at a criminal who flourishes in the face of those who would judge him; his refusal to take heed of social opprobrium is ultimately the source of his success. The state does not seem to regulate behavior, there does not appear to be an afterlife in which a supreme power might settle scores: there are no scales of justice to balance out his offenses. What is disgrace, then, if a scoundrel refuses to internalize society's values and evades punishment, only to grow richer and more successful? And what of the resemblance, impossible to miss, between the protagonist's name and that of Ghalib Halasa (1932–89), the Jordanian critic, activist, and novelist?

The title of the collection recalls the Arabic saying, "one who eats sour grapes will have their teeth dulled by acid," or in other words, we lie in a bed of our making. The element in *Sour Grapes* that unites humanity across cultures is the notion that we are, in the first instance, social creatures, our behavior exposed to and shaped by public scrutiny. Along with the craving of material wealth, of sensual pleasure that comes from food, sex and entertainment, the characters we encounter yearn for freedom, for a life lived without the unblinking eye of the police state and its informants, or the haughty scorn of neighbors. Yet our desires must inevitably compete: alliances are exposed as fleeting and self-serving, while both the village and the city are landscapes for feuds, conspiracies, and betrayals. In "Abaya in the Alley" (*mula'a fi al-zuqaq*) successive bouts of violence rain down without warning on a well-meaning Samaritan, showcasing a cruel, rudderless world.

In such hostile social contexts, sexuality—especially female sexuality—is an arena in which power and social mores most clearly intersect. For Tamer, women are a source of endless fascination and conflicting impulses: they appear as "biting snake(s)," "strutting peacock(s)," or innocents. He does not exempt women from the feebleness, double talk, and hypocrisies exhibited by men; rather, he lampoons the immense energy men and women expend to demand public propriety from women. In "The Thickets" (*al-adghal*), a male character's sister is insulted, with the offender playing on the well-worn notion that a family's honor hangs on the requirement for women to be chaste. The protagonist is moved to violence at hearing the insult, only to realize, at the close of the tale, that he in fact is an only child. Much of the narration is devoted to the whispering voices of animals who urge the man to avenge the insult. This theme advances further into absurdity in "Men" (*rijal*), where repeated threats from a cuckolded husband fail to bring his wife to heel. Finally, at the close of this—one of the shortest stories in the collection—does the husband divorce his wife, but then only for forgetting to add salt to her cooking.

For all its universality, *Sour Grapes* is chiefly an indictment of the fate to which Syrians have been condemned, as multiple tales encode place names, social customs, cultural perspectives, and practices that index Syria specifically, and contemporary Arab life more broadly. The village of Queiq features in a number of the stories in this collection; Arabic names are commonly used, as are familiar elements of the Syrian landscape. Maysalun, the site of a battle between French forces and a small Syrian-Arab force is explicitly invoked. While the French triumphed and proceeded to march on Damascus, the Battle of Maysalun remains an important "symbol of heroic Arabic resistance, in the face of insurmountable odds, to European domination."[2]

2. Kamal Salibi, "Maysalūn," in *Encyclopaedia of Islam* (2nd ed.), ed. P. Bearman et al., accessed 7 July 2022. First published online: 2012.

In an interview co-conducted for *Al-Jazeera* by one of the translators of this collection, we learn that Tamer is self-taught, having left school at the age of thirteen to support his family, and a writer of wide renown.[3] Tamer tells his interviewers flatly, "Anyone can rule Syria, but not this regime." He achieved fame as a short-story writer and served as the editor of major literary journals in his native Syria, only to be dismissed for an editorial in which he made thinly veiled references to the repression of Hafez al-Assad's government. Artists and writers in al-Assad's Syria, where "everything belongs to the regime: newspapers, publishing houses, magazines" could only choose between capitulation and imprisonment. In 1981, Tamer moved his family to Oxford in the United Kingdom, where he currently lives in exile. From the pulpit of his Facebook page, *Al-Mihmaz* (The Horse Spur), he continues to publish his stories and assail the current Syrian leader, Bashar al-Assad, and his government. He is equally disdainful of prominent Syrian opposition figures and their decadence, labeling them "clowns" and "peacocks."[4]

3. Franco Galdini and Alessandro Columbu, "Zakaria Tamer: 'On the Side of the Syrian People,'" *Al Jazeera*, 30 Aug. 2017.

4. Bashar al-Assad, an ophthalmologist by training, is the younger son of Hafez al-Assad, for whom the constitution was amended so that he might assume the presidency after his father's death.

The existential notion that our world lacks any overarching, transcendental truth crystallizes in the final tale in *Sour Grapes*, "The Last Story." A soporific storyteller in a café suddenly devises a new tale. He lulls his listless audience to sleep. Then, all of creation falls asleep, including "the brother who was interested in killing his own brother." The world reverts to a primordial state as they doze, where birds nest on cars and lay their eggs on the wings of planes. In this vision of our existence, our reality is the sum total of our conduct toward one another, born of free will; without the societies we've woven into being, animals reign over a world in which the signs of civilization blur to erosion. In a world lacking universal truths—except the assurance of our own deaths—there is only the disordered and cutthroat world of our own making.

The short stories for which the author is best known are hardly pious; the hypocrisies of the outwardly devout and the absurdities of blind faith are prime targets. In a tale entitled "Heaven" (*al-janna*), a docile and unquestioning believer obeys earthly and divine edicts with the same devotion. His reward—on this earth—at the age of sixty-five, is to become a camel in the desert, "chased around by female camels." Paradise, seen with the storyteller's jaundiced eye, comes as liberation from human existence; an uncritical mind finds its consummation in beastly bliss. And yet *Sour Grapes* opens with a quote from the Quran: "He said, 'O my son, do not relate your vision to your brothers.'" (12:5) In Sura Yusuf (Joseph), the chapter contains a warning about the betrayals of humankind—beware those who would betray you—while it offers hope by reminding the believer that God doesn't forsake us. For this reason, prisoners read it for comfort; the Quran cannot be banned in prison.[5] The sura itself declares its revelation "the best of stories." Islamic tradition considers it the most beautiful of stories because of "its wealth of matter, in which prophets, angels, devils, djinn, men, animals, birds, rulers and subjects play a part."[6] While the stories collected here also teem with earthly and supernatural figures, what might we make of the apparent parallel between "the best of stories" and Tamer's irreverent dreamscapes? What of the consolations of a higher power, an ultimate form of justice, that *Sour Grapes* withholds?

Thanks to Tamer and his able translators, we must confront our world unflinchingly, in all its oppression, sanctimoniousness and corruption. With such a gloomy catalogue of images seared into our minds, as we are held rapt by the echoing screams, we may look to Tamer's collection *The Land of Misery* (2015) for the next horizon:

5. I'm grateful to Elliott Colla for this insight.
6. Bernard Heller, "Yūsuf b. Yaʻḳūb," in *Encyclopaedia of Islam* (1st ed.), 1913–36, ed. M. Th. Houtsma et al., accessed 23 June 2022. First published online: 2012.

Poor words, they're nothing
    [. . . .]
They have neither pickaxes nor firepower to
besiege the palaces of tyrants
    And yet they alone can exhort the oppressed
to demand their lost freedom
    and to die for the sake of it[7]

Nader K. Uthman
Cambridge, Massachusetts

7. Zakariyya Tāmer. *Arḍ al-wayl [The Land of Misery]* (1st ed.) (Jadāwil lil-Nashr wa-al-Tarjamah wa-al-Tawzīʿ [Jadawel Press for Publishing, Translation and Distribution], 2015), p. 15.

Sour Grapes

The Quarrel

The Queiq neighborhood was notorious for its wealthy residents, who were so greedy that they would kill their mothers for more money. Queiq was also famous for its unruly children who sat in cafés and smoked shisha, and when they attacked other neighborhoods, no windowpane stood any chance of remaining intact against their rocks. No hawker dared to enter their neighborhood, for he would come out carrying the vegetables on his back himself instead of his mule's. If only they had learned their lessons in school as accurately as they had learned profanity, they would have been the smartest pupils in the entire world.

The Queiq neighborhood also owed its reputation to its rough men, who would never say no to a bloody fight and would happily go to prison. Men such as Khidr Alloun, who cut off his left ear in court in front of the judge and ate it with great pleasure; or Jasim al-Qazzaz, who would steal anything, even the kohl from a woman's eyes; or Mahmoud al-Jisr, whose knife moaned in distress for the many bodies it had stabbed.

The women of the Queiq were notorious for being so fearless and cocky, so fierce and impudent, that any sense of shame had long since abandoned them. Umm Ali was the most famous amongst them, although she was just a poor old widow. Her husband had died, leaving her with a single daughter that grew up to become the most attractive girl in the neighborhood, the one all the bachelors desired. Yet, none of them would dare to propose and have Umm Ali as their mother-in-law, as she was a woman that, had she been born male, would have spent her entire life in jail.

One day at noon, Umm Ali was walking through the souk of Queiq with a sulking face, with her head held high, moving along at a fast pace that didn't sit well with her age. Abu Salim, the neighborhood's barber, emerged from his shop and rushed to catch up with her, calling to her in a panting voice: "Umm Ali! Sister!"

Umm Ali stopped when she heard his voice, turned around as though a scorpion stung her and she snapped at him: "Are you not ashamed to talk to a woman you don't know? And who told you that I'm your sister and you're my brother? It would be beneath me to have a barber like you as my brother."

Abu Salim replied, "There is no power and no strength without God, allow me to say something briefly."

Umm Ali interrupted him. "Don't worry, I will only shave my beard at your shop when it grows!" she said sarcastically.

"This morning I went to Najib Bey al-Baqqar," said Abu Salim, "and I shaved him."

"Did you? Congratulations! What an honor!" said Umm Ali with a disgusted smirk.

Abu Salim said, "The Bey would like to see you to discuss an urgent matter."

"Al-Baqqar?" asked Umm Ali, "Isn't he the one who's always drunk?"

"We're not his mother," said Abu Salim trying to conceal his irritation, "the Lord will judge him on the last day."

"And what does His Highness the Bey want from me?" Umm Ali enquired.

"I have no idea," said Abu Salim, "I am merely delivering the message to you, as a messenger that's my only responsibility."

As Abu Salim rushed back into his shop, Umm Ali resumed her fast-paced walk, wondering what Najib al-Baqqar—the wealthiest man in the neighborhood—could possibly want from her. Her curiosity grew as she was walking by Najib al-Baqqar's stately house and she found herself knocking on the door. She told the maid that the Bey had asked to see her, and the maid showed her to the guest room before dashing out. It was a few minutes before Najib al-Baqqar appeared, greeting Umm Ali as though she were an old childhood friend with whom he always played with as a kid. He asked her to sit down and sat across from her. He inquired with interest about her health and that of her daughter's, but Umm Ali cut him short in reproach: "Listen, I don't have time to chatter with you. Cut the small talk and tell me what this is about."

"I know you're a poor woman in need," said Najib al-Baqqar slowly, weighing every single word carefully.

"I didn't come to your house to beg," Umm Ali said.

"By God, no!" Najib al-Baqqar interrupted her.

"What do you want from me then?" asked Umm Ali impatiently.

"Do you know Khidr Alloun?"

"Who doesn't? I know him and I know that people in this neighborhood are scared of his brutality and avoid him, but I am not scared of him, I can't stand the ground he walks on, and I can't stand his hideous looks."

Najib al-Baqqar's face brightened with joy as he said to Umm Ali, "We agree then, I can't stand the sight of that arrogant idiot. I would love to see him humiliated before I die, and no one in this neighborhood is more suitable than you for the task. I will give you anything you ask for."

Najib Bey al-Baqqar took out a wad of banknotes from his pocket and offered it to Umm Ali, who said: "No, no . . . I will put Khidr Alloun to shame for free."

"I like your reaction," said Najib Bey al-Baqqar, "You would be doing me a great service, which I wouldn't forget."

He picked up one more wad of banknotes and added it to the other one "Would you like something to drink? Tea or coffee?" he asked.

"I don't have time for trivialities," she grumbled.

As expected, a few days later, when Umm Ali and Khidr Alloun met face to face in the neighborhood's busy souk, she provoked him derisively. As Khidr Alloun barked at her "Get out of my way, woman!" all hell broke loose and he was bewildered at Umm Ali's cataclysmic reaction, angry but unable to do anything. It wouldn't have been appropriate for a man like him to hit a woman, so he silently swallowed the insults to him and his family, to his past, present, and future. His face went livid, but he bowed his head and didn't utter a single word.

That night, people in the neighborhood expected Umm Ali's house to be burned down by unknown men, but nothing happened; they thought someone would kidnap and rape her beautiful daughter, and return her to her mother's house naked, but she roamed the neighborhood as usual with the grace of a gazelle; they anticipated some mysterious accident to bring about Umm Ali's ruin, but nothing happened, she remained safe and sound, and her loud and resentful vituperations could still be heard around in the neighborhood.

The fact that she didn't have a son was a source of frustration that Umm Ali tried hard to conceal. She adored her sister's son Sulayman, a friendly boy in the prime of life. Had she had a son of her own, Sulayman would still be her favorite. The boy accepted her insistent invitations and visited her every evening, as she would never let a day pass without seeing him. One day, Sulayman called in to see her as usual and spent the evening at her place, but as she bid him farewell and was standing by the window following his leave from the house with an affectionate look, she saw the silhouette of a man resembling Khidr Alloun attacking him with his dagger and stabbing him repeatedly. The boy cried and screamed. "Please, sir, I beg of you!" the boy said to his murderer, who didn't pay attention to his blood pouring and to his lamentations and kept stabbing Sulayman with increasing brutality. Umm Ali's lungs ran out of breath and, for the first time in her life, she experienced the glacial thrill of fright. She wanted to cry, scream, and wail, but she choked and collapsed like a glass crashing against the hard ground, smashing into scattered tiny pieces. In the hospital, they didn't let her see Sulayman's stabbed body, which they said looked like a sieve with many holes.

Khidr Alloun said to the police that, at the time of the incident, he was spending the evening with a group of twenty men, who testified in his favor and confirmed that he didn't leave their table for a second. Najib al-Baqqar organized a dinner party to which more than fifty men were invited to celebrate Khidr Alloun's discharge from an unfair accusation that would have likely resulted in his hanging or in a life sentence.

Umm Ali marched in Sulayman's funeral wearing black clothes that she swore never to take off. She saw the gravedigger carrying Sulayman's corpse wrapped in his shroud and then lowering it into the gloomy grave. She was unable to shed a single tear and became just a flaccid chunk of meat that couldn't stop moaning and rattling, stumbling through the streets of Queiq with wandering glances, her back bent and her head dangling between her shoulders, indifferent to her neighbors' malicious looks. She would visit Sulayman's grave and sit for hours among the graves, listening in shock and wonder to invisible voices that only she could hear and that made her cry even more.

What happened in Queiq rid its people of their fear of Umm Ali and persuaded many men to ask for her daughter's hand.

Death of a Dagger

Khidr Alloun's mother was getting on her son's nerves with her raving about the latest developments in plastic surgery.

"So, you want to be a girl in her twenties again?" he asked her sarcastically.

"These operations are no good for people like me," his mother said to him, "but they could help someone like you. Today you could get a new ear to replace the one you foolishly cut off."

Khidr looked at his mother in resentment as she carried on, "You're over forty now, and you're still a bachelor. Others have married once or twice already, and some even three times. Who's going to marry you so long as you remain one-eared? All the men in our neighborhood have two ears, only you have one!"

"Who told you I'm ashamed of my ear? I actually take pride in it," said Khidr with vanity and great confidence.

"You know," his mother said, "women in our neighborhood have forgotten your name. They call you Mr. Cut-off Ear!"

"I'm a man," said Khidr, "I'm indifferent to what little, low-minded women have to say."

Antara Ibn Shaddad secretly accompanied Khidr day and night.

"Don't listen to your mother's nonsense," said Antara to Khidr. "My enemies used to speak ill of me for my black complexion, but I remained the man that Abla loved, and that all the men revered and sought to please."

"Please, Khidr, in God's name. You don't know what's in a mother's heart," said his mother in a genuine tone. "All children, even monkey-like ones, look like beautiful gazelles to their mothers. I only want the best for you, and I see you as the most beautiful man in the world. But you just have to look at yourself in the mirror to realize I'm not kidding you. You look terrible. You neglect yourself as though you were an orphan, you shave your hair completely to look bald, you let your moustache grow and don't care about your clothes. And your ear is ripped off."

"If you let your mother talk," said Antara Ibn Shaddad, "the next thing she will suggest is that you get your hair cut in a woman's salon."

Khidr looked at his mother and he felt pity for her. She was in her sixties, but her face was so creased by her wrinkles that she looked like she was ninety. She seldom laughed.

She sighed and said to him, "Make me happy before I die, Khidr. I'm old and I will die soon. When will I become a grandmother and see my grandchildren?"

"Right! Don't you already have an army of grand-children?" replied Khidr. "My sister is married and has five scoundrels."

"But those are the children of a stranger, not your children," said his mother.

"It has become fashionable these days for men to emulate women," said Antara Ibn Shaddad to Khidr, "and for women to emulate men. Only few men are real men these days, and nobody understands them."

His mother was shocked to see her son laughing. He'd been frowning and looking so angry, as if he were about to explode. She said to him impatiently: "May God help you and your twisted mind."

He kissed his mother's hand and left her house to head over to the local café. He sat down alone, smoking his shisha. Antara Ibn Shaddad said to him, "Don't smile. When men smile too much they become like coquettish women."

The frown on Khidr Alloun's face deepened, and patrons sitting at nearby tables moved away from him, fearing a fierce fight was about to break out. At that point, two cops entered the café, and one of them bellowed out to the patrons to stand up and raise their hands. They started searching everyone and found Khidr Alloun in possession of a sharp dagger.

One of the two cops took the dagger out of its sheath and questioned Khidr in a reproaching voice: "Don't you know that it's prohibited to carry weapons?"

Khidr vaguely stammered some indefinable words, but the other cop poked him and said, "Stop talking from your nose. The gentleman asked you a question and you will answer him. Why are you carrying a dagger?"

"Because I like fruit," said Khidr.

"What a sorry excuse!" said the cop.

"The doctor asked me specifically to peel the fruit before eating it," said Khidr.

The two officers burst out laughing and did not arrest Khidr, but they confiscated his dagger and suggested that he should eat his fruit without peeling it in order not to incur sanctions in the future.

Khidr sat down dumbfounded, feeling ashamed, as though he were naked. "A man who gives up on his knife isn't a man and he only deserves to sit among women," said Antara Ibn Shaddad to Khidr.

"But it's the coppers who took it!" said Khidr.

"As if you didn't know that they are people too!" replied Antara Ibn Shaddad. "They are human beings like you and me who will die one day, just like you and me."

"Without my dagger, I'm as fragile as an old, paralyzed woman," said Khidr.

"How is your dagger going to return into your possession?" Antara asked him.

Khidr pondered silently, then he suddenly sprang from his chair and left the café hastily. He rushed over to the wealthiest and most influential man in the neighborhood. He met with Najib al-Baqqar, and his voice trembled as he spoke: "Look, Najib Bey, everyone in this neighborhood at some point has come to you with their requests. I'm the only one who's never asked anything from you."

"That's correct," said Najib, "and I must say, I thought you hated me."

"I've come today to ask something from you," said Khidr, "so don't turn me down."

"Ask me anything," said Najib, "your request will be fulfilled instantly, inshallah."

Khidr was choking on his own words as he told Najib what had just occurred at the café. He asked Najib earnestly to intercede for him to recover his knife, especially since Najib was friends with the chief of police and he wouldn't say no to him.

Najib contemplated the situation briefly, then said to Khidr, "Why don't you buy a new knife? I will buy you a knife you can cut rocks with!"

"I appreciate your generosity," replied Khidr stubbornly, "but I've been friends with my knife for ages, I want it back."

"I will talk to the chief of police today," said Najib, "everything will play out just the way you wish."

The next morning, Khidr ran to Najib al-Baqqar's home and found him still in his pajamas, stretching and yawning. "So, Bey? What happened?" asked Khidr impatiently.

Najib said he was sorry, but it seemed that one of the officers sold the knife to a foreign female tourist whom he didn't know. The police considered what the cop did a misdemeanor, and he would be punished for it, but Najib suggested that Khidr forget his dagger. Khidr shouted: "How can I forget it? Are you aware that I've had that knife since I was ten? Do you know that I put it under my pillow at night? And that when I'm in prison, it's torturing for me to be away from it?"

"There is nothing you can do about it," said Najib "even our dearest friends have to die, think of your knife as a departed friend."

Khidr replied in a reproachful tone: "Of all people, never would I have expected this from someone like you, from a man who knows what it means to be a man."

Khidr left Najib's house fuming and wandered about the neighborhood feeling agitated. He daydreamed of his knife calling to him and recalled how he shivered in ecstasy every time he felt its blade or clutched its handle. He was confident that even if someone tossed it into a bottomless well, his knife would jump out to reach as high as mountain tops.

"If I had to choose between Abla and my sword," said Antara, "I wouldn't hesitate a second. I would choose my sword, for a man without his weapon is like a woman doomed to get raped."

Khidr Alloun felt vulnerable, like a helpless game in the jungle. He felt the need to breath fresh air, a different air. He left the neighborhood and walked leisurely on a broad street covered with asphalt, punctuated on either side by green trees and tall, white buildings. Suddenly a fast car hit him and ran him over. He was taken to a hospital nearby, but he died at dawn the day after. As he was drawing his last breath, Antara said to him: "You have no regrets, don't be sorry. You can die peacefully."

The men of the Queiq neighborhood walked in Khidr Alloun's funeral preceded by Antara Ibn Shaddad, who led them with a bowed head. Khidr Alloun was proud to see Antara take part in his burial ceremony. He was sorry, though, to realize that his neighbors could not see Antara piling up earth onto his dead friend with his sword.

The Night Singer

It was almost midnight. Shafiq al-Kawa had been singing and playing his oud tirelessly, song after song, in front of a crowd of men who came to Masoud al-Asfar's house accepting his generous invitation to an evening that would end at dawn when the Adhan called for the morning prayer. The evening was one of music entertainment, delicious food, different types of wine, and cigarettes stuffed with tobacco and weed. They ate the dinner leisurely, drank copious glasses of wine, smoked cigarettes, and conversed loudly. Every once in a while, Masoud al-Asfar would welcome them once again, asking them to eat without shame as if they were in their homes. Even though Shafiq al-Kawa wasn't enjoying the evening, he continued to play the oud and sang until, all of a sudden, the strings of the oud for some reason snapped and he stopped singing. Everybody turned to him, staring at him keenly. Masoud al-Asfar rushed to him, concerned.

Shafiq said to him calmly, "Rest assured! I will try to sing without the oud."

Masoud replied, objecting, "But we agreed that you would play the lute and sing. If you only sing, I will only pay you half your fee."

Shafiq grumbled, but he said to Masoud: "All I care about now is that your guests are happy."

"Wow!" bellowed one of the drunken guests, "his voice was already unbearable alongside the oud. He even missed a few notes. Imagine if it were just his voice alone!"

Another man yelled, "I will sing better than him and for free."

A third man shouted, "I am ready to sing too, and I will pay anything to anybody tough enough to be patient to listen to my voice."

And a fourth man exclaimed: "What is the real name of the singer . . . Shafiq al-Kawa or Shafiq al-Bow-wow?"

The guests' laughter and clamor grew louder. Shafiq was outraged and as he pointed at the men. He said to Masoud: "Unless the brothers stop mocking me and my voice, I'm afraid I will have to leave your house."

Masoud answered him with a sarcastic voice, "No regret, no sorrow! You know where the door is, right?"

Shafiq al-Kawa took his lute and left. He walked through dark alleyways to get home, cursing these miserable times and the humiliation of having to sing to a group of dumb, drunken men. Once at home, he wanted to restring his lute, but he could not find any new strings. He stood in front of a long mirror and started to sing faintly, though it did not take long before he raised his voice and got carried away. He was interrupted by a messenger from the Caliph, who came to his house and asked him to appear immediately in front of His Majesty to sing for him. Shafiq declined his offer, stating that he swore to sing only for beggars. Later, the Caliph came to visit him unaccompanied. He sat down on the large carpet on the floor and implored Shafiq to sing for him, but Shafiq persisted: "I will only sing for beggars." The Caliph replied to him with a smile: "Are you blind? Can't you see that now I'm not the Caliph of Muslims, but a beggar desperate for a little bit of amusement?"

The Caliph sighed and told Shafiq about the gloomy feelings, the unbearable misery and distress he suffered every night. He was devastated since the only woman he loved had fallen in love with one of his slaves and abandoned him. Shafiq felt pity for him and eventually agreed to sing for him. "I'm all ears," said the Caliph.

Shafiq sang and the Caliph felt enraptured. He asked for an encore and Shafiq carried on prodigally. He sang for hours until the Caliph called out to Shafiq and begged him to stop singing for a bit lest his heart would stop beating from too much happiness, joy, and ecstasy. He couldn't take any more. Shafiq stopped playing and listened at length to the Caliph heaping praise on him. The Caliph asked Shafiq if he would like to become his Kingdom's prime singer and number one music authority. Shafiq was going to answer when he heard a loud knock on the door. He looked at the Caliph, wondering what to do, and the Caliph granted him permission. Shafiq opened the door to a policeman with a frown on his face who told him that his neighbors had called the police station to complain. They claimed that a man was being brutally beaten in his house and was crying for help in sheer agony.

Shafiq, baffled, angrily denied the allegations of the neighbors, and said to the policeman: "After my mother's death, no one has lived in this house but me. You can confirm it yourself. Come inside . . . make yourself at home."

The officer entered the house and carried out a meticulous and detailed inspection of the room, but he found neither the perpetrator nor the victim of the alleged beating and he scowled as he left the house, feeling sorry for those who had to endure liars as their neighbors.

Grey Day

Shukri al-Mubayyid and his fellow inmates performed dangerous exercises to stay in good shape, often resulting in injuries, contusions, bruises, and wounds to their bodies. Roasting his favorite delicacy, chestnut, was Shukri's hobby, which often resulted in burns to his hands, his feet, his back, his chest, and his stomach.

One morning, Shukri al-Mubayyid was shaving his beard while he listened to the news and music on the radio. However, his right hand made a mistake when gripping the razor and, instead of removing the useless hair from his face, it slit his throat with a reckless movement, ripping it from side to side. Shukri al-Mubayyid was transferred to the best hospital where the doctors tried to fix him but to no avail. His body was placed in a sturdy bag and handed over to a car that on a daily basis distributed the dead to their families. It wasn't too difficult for the driver to find his way to Shukri al-Mubayyid's house in the Queiq neighborhood, but he found out to his surprise that the house had been empty for months. Shukri's father was arrested for vagrancy and begging. His brother was being prosecuted for stealing state funds. His mother was imprisoned for verbally violating the honor of the most respectable women, and his sister had been detained because she deliberately doesn't express her joy or sadness.

The driver asked the neighbors about his relatives. They told him that Shukri's paternal uncle had emigrated to America and his maternal uncle, along with his sons and daughters, had moved to Canada. His cousin had also emigrated to Australia and his maternal aunt was working as a maid in Dubai. The driver then asked for the addresses of Shukri's friends, but all those who were said to be his friends swore with pale faces that they were not his mates, they had never exchanged a word with him, and if they ran into him, they wouldn't recognize him.

Shukri al-Mubayyid was embarrassed and took the driver's off-guard moment as an opportunity to flee and go buy vegetables and fruit that his wife had asked him to get. He hid in his family's house, waiting for his relatives to come back and to bury him, cheerfully trilling in celebration of his release from prison.

Men

Abd al-Halim al-Murr swore that he would divorce his wife Nabila if she dared to leave the house by herself without his permission, and so Nabila started going out every day and he got angry. He swore that he would divorce her if she dared to walk on the street without the hijab, but Nabila took it off and started using it to clean the floor, and he got angry. He swore that he would divorce her if she ever spoke to any other man but him. One afternoon, he came home from work unexpectedly and he found her on the bed talking to a man he had never seen before, and he got angry. He swore that he would divorce her if he found out that that same man was the reason behind her swollen belly. Nabila laughed and explained to him that the fat food she made produced gas that can fly a hot-air balloon. A few months later, though, she gave birth to a girl and Abd al-Halim got angry, and he swore he would divorce her if she gave birth to another girl. However, he only divorced her after a few weeks because she forgot to put salt in the food she cooked.

The Rain

Nayla was standing in the courtyard of the house humming a melancholic song, holding a glassy jug filled with water, watering the roses when the doorbell rang insistently. She rushed to open the door to find one of her husband's young employees who told her with a broken, terrified voice that her husband, Kazem al-Hamwi, fainted in his store and an ambulance took him to the hospital but he died before arriving there. The jug slipped out of her fingers and fell to the ground, smashing into pieces. She opened her eyes wide, disoriented and astonished. Grief paralyzed her and didn't let her cry, scream, shout, or hit her face and chest. A feeling of distress made her sit on the cold floor, ignoring the comfortable chair that was right next to her. Suddenly, a feeling of humility overwhelmed her, she prostrated to the ground and kissed it. Then she looked up to the sky and screamed out: "You are great, o Lord!"

When she sat on the floor, Nayla was merely a thirty-year-old woman but, almost as if there were a certain enigmatic magic to tragedies, when she stood up, she looked like a teenager and her skin tone went from yellow to rosy. She rushed to the kitchen and poured oil, butter, and vinegar into the sink. She threw the bulgur, rice, lentils, peppers, thyme, and salt on the floor, as though food had lost its taste after her husband's death. Next, she left the kitchen and dashed through the rooms to gather all her husband's clothes. She cut them into small pieces with a pair of scissors, threw them into the courtyard of the house, and burned them. She destroyed all her husband's photographs, as she believed images were blasphemous. She deleted a dangerous page full of sins from her husband's archive in the hereafter.

The devastating grief made her forget to put on her black abaya and she marched, leaving her head uncovered behind the coffin where her husband's body laid wrapped in a shroud. Nayla's long black hair hung loosely over her shoulders and her face, flying in the wind. She didn't buy a black dress for the occasion because she was determined to give all her husband's money to charity. She just wore a short, tight red dress that would not reach her milky-colored knees no matter how much she stretched it. She walked slowly in a dignified manner, a walk that could make men melancholy and sleepless. When the funeral reached the cemetery and the coffin was lowered into the grave's pit and buried under the earth, Nayla lost her composure and started trilling cries of joy, believing she was actually wailing. She shouted at him in anguish: "How could you leave me, Kazem?"

Her husband, Kazem al-Hamwi, had no family of his own. He was a rich man who didn't trust banks and banknotes. He turned everything he made into gold coins, which he hid in different secret places in his house that Nayla knew very well. He owned a big store that sold all types of fabrics, including the most expensive ones. Nayla went on to sell everything hastily, as if she was planning to travel soon, although she didn't. She refused to live in a house that had witnessed her and her husband's relatively comfortable lives and decided to sell it, too. She bought a larger and fancier house that could accommodate her memories with her husband and furnished it thoroughly. Men, married and single, kept going to the house to offer their condolences to a woman who would never forget her dead husband.

The First Round

Alaa al-Salat didn't lose hope and wooed Saada al-Malli for months, giving her looks of passionate love and sending her secret perfumed letters until she agreed to meet him outside the neighborhood on a street far from curious eyes. From the very first moment of their date, he rushed to hold her hand, squeezed it and blushed. They exchanged looks and he appeared to her as the most charming and attractive young man. She seemed to him the prettiest of girls. He told her that he loved her more than he loved roast chicken, which made her half-close her eyes. Despite the embarrassment, she said to him in a faint tone that she had loved him at first sight more than she loved Farid al-Atrash's songs.

"Are you joking?" asked Alaa in astonished disapproval. "How can you listen to his songs? In all my life, I couldn't listen to a single one. They are all cheesy."

His words irked Saada, "His songs are not cheesy, they touch the heart and only a sensitive, cultivated person can appreciate them."

He released her hand and asked her resentfully, "Are you suggesting that I'm dumb and heartless?"

Saada replied in a defiant tone, "Feel free to interpret my words the way you like."

Alaa was fuming. He said to her, "No woman can insult Alaa al-Salat."

Saada looked as if she was preparing to slap him. "No man can insult Saada al-Malli either," she threatened him.

Saada imagined Alaa sitting day and night behind a table wolfing down roast chicken, gasping loudly, and dripping with sweat. Alaa imagined Saada listening to Farid al-Atrash and that whenever he asked her a question, she would answer with a passage from one of his songs. He stared at her and saw a skinny girl with a big mouth, a dumb look in her eyes, and a yellow face that made him sick. She looked back at him and saw a bear disguised as a chubby young man, short, with two bent legs and algae-colored eyes, and they split in disgust and regret.

Day and Night

The morning paper announced that the minister of finance had resigned and the search for his successor had begun. Nawaf al-Homsi was delighted by this news. His nose, his hands, and his feet congratulated him, confident that if they wanted an honest man to do the job then he was the one they should choose. His right foot asked him about the first thing he would do, and he replied without hesitation: "I will ride around in the minister's car, sit on the minister's chair, and receive the minister's salary and all the secret presents a minister is entitled to."

His nose asked him what he would say in his first speech. "I've got many things to say," said Nawaf. "For starters, I don't like the current taxes and I will demand that they raise or lower them."

"What's with you, all silent? You would usually ask me a question, but you haven't," said Nawaf to his left foot.

His left foot said to Nawaf: "My only concern at the moment is your worn-out shoes, so what are you going to do?"

"I will go barefoot," said Nawaf. "No one will notice because they will all be busy looking at my face trying to figure out what I want and what I don't."

In the afternoon, Nawaf listened to the news, to find out that a new minister had been appointed whose name wasn't Nawaf al-Homsi. The books scattered around him in the room exulted, delighted to find out that he would be forced to remain with them; *Avarice and The Avaricious* by al-Jahiz, and *al-Ayyam* by Taha Hussein engaged in a fierce discussion, but Nawaf interrupted them with a loud scream, reminding them that books were made to be read and not to prattle; and *The Broken Wings* by Gibran Kahlil Gibran said in a defying tone: "Who's to tell the difference between reading and prattling?"

While Nawaf al-Homsi yawned indifferently, *The Book of Songs* by Fairuzabadi added, "If I were fire, I would burn all those books that don't respect the night in silence."

The Thief and the Dogs by Najib Mahfuz replied, "Don't think the number of your pages makes you intimidating, or that it gives you the right to threaten and bluster."

An authorless diwan of poetry added, "I would like to propose a minute of silence to mourn the victims of the earthquake in Colombia."

Nawaf dashed out of his room and left his house. He went to the offices of one of the newspapers to meet with the editor-in-chief, who greeted him warmly like a famous writer. The editor congratulated Nawaf on an article that he recently sent him, and which he enjoyed greatly for the original and courageous ideas it contained.

Nawaf blushed and said: "The only thing that matters is that the article be published as soon as possible, before the event I wrote about takes place."

"It's an honor for our paper to be able to publish it," said the editor, "but I'm sure you agree it still needs some minor editing."

"The pen is in my hand, and the article is in front of me," replied Nawaf.

"The title of the article is very original," said the editor, "but it's also provocative and ironic. As you know our paper maintains a low profile and we prefer ordinary titles."

"The title isn't a problem," said Nawaf, "it can be changed."

"Your article contains some harsh criticism of people that we are eager to be friends with," continued the editor, "that would be dangerous for all of us."

"I will remove the criticism," replied Nawaf.

"Not only that," said the editor, "they're people who deserve praise and commendation, a free mind like yours should not neglect to mention their achievements in the article."

"I will praise them instead of criticizing them then," said Nawaf.

"Your article is very long. Almost two-thousand words. We would appreciate it if you could summarize it in four-hundred words, or even less. You know how readers are these days, they get bored quickly."

Nawaf pondered briefly then asked the editor: "If I change the article following your remarks, what will remain?"

"Your name written in black large characters will remain," pointed out the editor, "as well as the remuneration that we will pay to you after its publication."

Nawaf bowed down to adjust the article, making it suitable to be published in the prestigious newspaper without saying a word. After successfully submitting the article to the editor, Nawaf went to an assembly that he was not allowed to miss and sat down with two old friends pretending to be listening to what the speakers had to say. His friend Ahmad sitting to his left poked his arm with his elbow and said to Nawaf in a bossy voice: "Clap, Nawaf, clap."

"I didn't hear anything worth clapping for," said Nawaf.

"Don't question and clap."

"I will clap if I want to."

"You will clap because you must clap."

Nawaf clapped with enthusiasm and his friend Darwish, sitting to his right, poked him too and told him to clap. Nawaf kept applauding until his palms were swollen, although he didn't know why. His friend Ahmad poked him again and then asked him: "What are you clapping for?"

"I'm clapping for the speakers."

"But there are no speakers behind the microphones."

"Maybe I'm clapping at the quality of the microphone."

"The microphone is imported from another country."

"Whereas clapping is a local product that makes your hands and arms stronger."

"The event is over, and we are the only ones in the hall."

"You are still clapping though."

"I'm clapping because a man sitting next to me poked my arm and told me to clap and asked me to tell you to clap too."

His friend Darwish, sitting on his right, poked him again and still clapping, asked him in surprise: "Why are you clapping?"

Darwish then poked his wife Amina and in a disapproving tone: "Why are you clapping?"

Amina stroked her belly affectionately and she laughed as she asked her baby who was still in the womb: "Why are you clapping?"

When Nawaf came home after midnight, the books in his room were silent. He was silent too and went to sleep. In his dreams, he saw himself swimming in space, kicking the planet earth until it crumbled into dust and torn meat.

Abaya in the Alley

If it hadn't been Muhsin al-Fayer's destiny to cross that narrow, winding alley in the Queiq neighborhood looking for a shortcut, right now he wouldn't be in this dark desolate pit. He could have walked gleefully under the bright sunshine. Or perhaps he could have relaxed in a coffee shop smoking shisha, laughing at his friends' conversations about mysterious, pretty, and sexy women. He could have lain on his bed listening to his younger brothers fighting and cursing each other.

Instead, he darted into that alley and was stopped by a woman wearing a black abaya who asked him in a soft, shy voice: "Brother, do you know where Hammoud al-Ghayeb's house might be?"

Muhsin said to her, "I have a friend named Abd al-Halim al-Ghayeb, but he doesn't live here."

"The house I want is Hammoud al-Ghayeb's house," replied the woman.

Right then, the door of one of the houses nearby opened and a young man emerged rushing hastily toward Muhsin, holding a large stick and yelling in disapproval: "Why you shameless! How dare you harass my sister?"

The woman with the black abaya quickly disappeared inside the house, looking at them with contempt, slamming the door behind her. Muhsin tried to calm the young man: "Listen, brother, listen to me . . ."

But the young man snapped at him: "Piss off! You are less than a quarter of a man whereas all my brothers are the manliest of men."

Muhsin's voice trembled as he said, "You don't understand, your sister stopped me to ask me about a house and I was answering her."

"Which one did she ask you about?" said the young man.

"Hammoud al-Ghayeb's," said Muhsin.

The young man laughed furiously and said to him, "I am Hammoud al-Ghayeb. Are you trying to convince me that my sister who lives with me forgot the house in which she was born?"

"I told you exactly what happened," said Muhsin. "Ask your sister."

"I know my sister, she is more decent than any woman in your family," said the young man.

Muhsin said, "I don't know what to say to convince you."

The young man was fuming: "Just admit that you are a scoundrel," he said to Muhsin. "You harass women, but you forget that women have men who protect them from perverts like you."

The young man bent over with his large stick to hit Muhsin's head with a harsh blow and Muhsin fell to the ground. His skull was fractured and it bled profusely. The young man kept beating him with his stick, hitting him repeatedly on the head. Muhsin regretted the whole thing; had that woman not approached him and he hadn't spoken to her, he would not have been laid out now in a cold ditch with his head crushed, unable to watch a boxing match on TV, whose result he was anxious to know.

The Holiday

Diab al-Ahmad was thankful for the great number of books in his home and was even more delighted when men, women, and children came out of their pages. They spoke to him, drank his coffee, smoked his cigarettes, ate his food, slept in his bed, and bathed in his bath. They looked into his memoirs, which were full of complaints and indignation. They tore their pages apart playfully and they made hats, boats, and planes out of them. They succeeded in luring him to leave with them to their green land. Later, the doctors carefully examined his motionless body and established that he was in a coma and that he would not wake up from it. However, they were surprised by the peaceful smile on his face.

The Divorced Woman

As the sun made everyone else run from the midday heat and hide inside their cool homes and cafés, a woman covered in black entered the graveyard. She was being followed by a short, stocky man with a stern face, who observed her as she walked between the graves until she stopped and sat down with her head and her back bent down. He approached her promptly and confidently, and asked her in a reproachful tone: "What are you doing?"

That question came unexpected, but she replied in an anxious voice, "Visiting my husband."

The man looked around with sarcastic eyes and asked, "Where is your husband?"

As she pointed to one of the graves, he asked her: "When did he die?"

"A year ago."

"A whole year without a man is an unbearable torture," said the man, feigning compassion.

The man looked around and saw the graveyard was empty. He jumped on the widow with a sudden move and threw her to the ground next to her husband's grave. She tried to scream and call for help, but his hand blocked her mouth harshly, while his other hand grabbed a knife and put it to her neck.

"I will slaughter you," she heard him saying in a threatening tone.

She begged him not to tear her clothes. "How will I manage to return to my house with my clothes all torn up?" she asked.

"The only clothes I'll tear cannot be seen when you're walking on the street."

The widow's husband was furious and urged her to resist until her last breath. He reminded her that respectable women would rather be slaughtered like sheep than surrender. Her answer came in the form of that familiar panting he heard frequently in the bedroom. She couldn't hear him as he told her in disdain that he divorced her.

Al-Hala's End

Jabir al-Maqsun took a yellow pill before delivering a mosque sermon in which he condemned the yellow pills that Said al-Hala', the barber, had been pushing, for they defied the Creator, who could have made all people rich, strong, happy, and free from illness if He wanted to. Ahmad al-Hatmi, a secondary school teacher, also took a yellow pill, sat in a café, and said to everyone around him in an angry loud voice that if Said al-Hala', the barber, really loved his neighborhood, he wouldn't exploit his neighbors' weakness for his profit, he would rather give out his yellow pills to his neighbors for free or at least at a discount.

Salim al-Habal, the man with the thickest moustache, also took a yellow pill on the sly as he proudly said to his drunken friends, as they staggered around in Samira the dancer's house, that a man is born a man and a barber cannot restore what time has marred.

The people of Queiq didn't pay much attention to the rumors surrounding the yellow pills but they all agreed on the amazing, remarkable, almost magical effect they had on people's minds and souls. These pills could impregnate the sterile, turn an impotent man into one capable of satisfying four women in one night, transform a coward into a brave daring man who roams around looking for his match in a fight. The yellow pills could turn dumb, lazy kids into hardworking, outstanding students with the highest marks in their exams, and they could fill the miserable, pitiful, and a submissive man with pride and glee. Now when they noticed their husbands standing upright with the haughtiness of a king, the wives of Queiq didn't have to look for an explanation because they knew they had become addicted to the yellow pills that Said al-Hala', the barber, was pushing.

As for Said al-Hala', his situation changed, and people now strove to please him after he had striven all his life to please them. He sent away his most loyal customers and he closed his shop. And who could really blame him? Everybody knew he was now making in a day more than he used to make in a year. He sat in his house confident that whoever wanted his pills would go to him, no matter where he was.

Rumor after rumor spread in the neighborhood about the effects and the origin of those pills, but the barber always pointed up with his finger and replied with a smile to whomever asked him about their origin. For months people watched Said al-Hala's moves closely but to no avail. They only became more dumbfounded. He sat in his house, hugging his little son or his wife. No one suspicious visited him. In fact, nobody visited him at all. He didn't get any mail, neither letters nor parcels, and he didn't buy anything that could possibly be used as ingredients for the production of pills. He would never disclose to anyone where they came from, how they were made, who made them, and what the ingredients were.

Said al-Hala's wife's friends also tried to talk her into revealing how her husband got his hands on the pills, except that she knew as much as everyone else in the neighborhood. All she could tell them was that Said al-Hala' insisted that she didn't take the pills because he liked her the way she was and didn't want her to be the way she wanted to be.

A delegation of merchants and tradesmen even met with Said al-Hala' and presented him with very tempting plans for the production of the pills and their marketing everywhere in the country, to which Said al-Hala' replied by saying that his pills were exclusively for his neighborhood. Import–export experts met with him and offered to commercialize his pills around the world and realize great profits, but he refused and disapproved angrily saying that those profits would be immoral.

Resentment against Said al-Hala' arose and quickly spread in the neighborhood when all differences disappeared between the smart and the dumb, the strong and the weak. The resentment became sharper and stronger when men who had a reputation for being wimp and submissive started confronting men known for their strength, their courage, and their bravery, turning them into a laughingstock.

They laid their blame on no one but Said al-Hala'
and his pills. He was found dead near his house one
day, his body bearing signs of torture, but nobody
knew who killed him. After his death, the yellow pills
vanished from Queiq. The stupid went back to being
stupid, the wimp to being wimp, and the miserable to
being miserable.

What a Pity!

Jasim al-Qazzaz was escorted into the prison courtyard. He saw the prison director's wife standing by the door of her husband's office, talking to him and laughing. Jasim wished to get into bed with her. She was a mature woman, like a ripe peach in August, like a horse that neighs unheard, eager to be tamed. However, the guard nudged his rifle to Jasim's back and barked at him: "Keep walking, you shameless pervert."

The guard took Jasim to a cell where ten other men had been serving long sentences, the shortest of which was seven years. A prisoner with a thick moustache and a frowning face asked him the reason of his incarceration, to which Jasim answered immediately: "Murder."

"Who did you kill?" the prisoner said to him. "A pot of zucchini stuffed with fine rice and chopped lamb?"

Though that question took him by surprise, Jasim answered the prisoner with a smile: "I killed a cop."

The prisoner patted Jasim on the shoulder and said: "Lying is forbidden and strongly frowned upon here. The guard who accompanied you saw your file and told us everything before we were honored with your presence."

Jasim stood his ground and said: "True, I stole something, but I was also going to kill the cop who arrested me."

The prisoner replied, "And what did you steal? Don't lie."

Jasim sighed and answered: "I was walking in my neighborhood on my way to the mosque to pray the Midday prayer in congregation . . ."

The prisoner interrupted him, saying: "Were you going to steal everyone's shoes?"

The cell filled with the prisoners' laughter, which bothered Jasim and made him go silent. The prisoner asked him to finish his story.

"I've forgotten what I was saying," said Jasim.

The prisoner said to him: "Let me remind you of the first bit—you were walking . . ."

Jasim continued, "I was walking, and the smell of some delicious food made me lose my mind. The smell came from behind a door left ajar. I pushed the door a little bit and I saw a pot of zucchini left on the fire in the middle of a courtyard in an otherwise empty house. So, I bolted in, picked up the pot and left the house. On my way out, I noticed a woman, a malicious girl, screeching: 'Thief!' He's running away . . ."

The prisoner asked him eagerly: "And the pot of zucchini?"

Jasim answered, "I was carrying it carefully not to spill the broth and then I found myself surrounded by a group of men who were not from my neighborhood. One of them was a cop who tried to arrest me, so I hit him."

"With what did you hit him?" the prisoner asked him inquisitively. "With a stuffed zucchini?"

The prisoners burst out laughing again. Jasim went cross and swore not to speak again.

"I have one last question for you," the inmate asked him. "What happened to the zucchini?"

"I won't say a word," said Jasim.

The prisoner asked him, "Did you present the pot of zucchini to the court as hard evidence?"

"I won't say a word" Jasim reiterated.

The prisoner patted him on the shoulder: "You are going to be our guest for a long time. Eventually you will talk, even just to listen to your own voice. That way you won't forget how to speak."

"My trial is tomorrow, and I will be acquitted," said Jasim.

The prisoner, while stroking his moustache, said: "I swear I will shave my moustache if they let you go."

The next morning, Jasim al-Qazzaz was taken to the courtroom handcuffed. His wife Badea was waving at him along with ten young children of different ages who had come along with her. When Jasim saw them, his eyes filled with tears, though he resorted to all his manliness trying not to cry. He was also staggering, although people could barely notice. He made an effort to regain his composure and appeared in front of the judge. He bent his head slightly and talked as though he was a cheerful child who had had a life of grief since the day he saw his mother die. He was embarrassed and confessed what he had done, adding that he did not steal a car, a building, or a bank; he only stole to feed his hungry children. His index finger shook as he pointed to the corner where his wife and children were standing. The children broke into tears, crying quite loud. The judge was confused and ordered their mother to silence the kids. The mother tried to calm them down, but their tears made her cry too. The judge frowned and looked like he wanted to make a decision quickly. He pronounced his verdict, sentencing him to pay a fine of an amount equal in value to what he had tried to steal and advised him not to steal again, even when his children were hungry. He ordered his release and once Jasim was no longer in handcuffs, he ran to his wife and his children, who formed a circle around him, clinging to him and cheerfully shrieking: "Papa! Papa!"

Jasim al-Qazzaz left the courtroom with his wife and the children. He ran into an old friend, with whom he shook hands, hugged, kissed, and they engaged in a long conversation. His wife, tired of waiting, rushed to return the ten children to their respective families, as she had borrowed them for a reasonable price for four hours, promising she would return them before five o'clock. Jasim returned to his house later and carried on with his life the way he had been used to. The moon did not rise that night as expected. People in the neighborhood were upset and puzzled, they whispered to each other, and they eyed Jasim al-Qazzaz warily, but the moon did emerge after all to dissipate any doubts.

Later, when Jasim and his wife Badea were having dinner after midnight as usual, he told her wondering, "Did you know, Badea, that my imprisonment is a lesson for you?"

Badea was baffled. "I did not go to jail," she said to him laughing. "How can this be a lesson for me?"

Jasim replied, "If I had left the house full enough, I wouldn't have been tempted by the pot of zucchini."

Badea was thinking about what he had just said when Jasim asked her: "Are you OK?"

"Oh, that's odd!" answered Badea. "Wasn't prison a lesson for you to repent for your theft?"

Jasim said, "Certainly. I would rather rob a bank next time, so long as the punishment is the same."

"I have never entered a bank in my life . . . What would you steal from it?" Badea inquired.

Jasim said, "Thousands of dollars, or hundreds of thousands, or thousands of thousands."

"We will buy a car!" answered Badea with great joy.

Jasim said, "Walking is better for your health."

"We will buy a new house!" Badea went on.

"It would be disgraceful to leave the house where we married," Jasim replied.

Badea said, "We will move to an upscale neighborhood!"

"God forbid!" Jasim thundered as he stood up frowned.

Banks, buildings, and shops were robbed but Jasim al-Qazzaz did not steal anything. Then, two spoons were stolen from a restaurant where Jasim was a regular costumer. He was arrested, interrogated mercilessly, and then they took him to court and transferred him to prison. He was received by the ugly prisoner with the moustache, who proceeded to ask him: "What did you do this time?"

"They unfairly accused me of stealing a spoon," answered Jasim.

The prisoner said to him: "And you are innocent. You did not steal it, did you?"

"Why would I steal a spoon when I have been eating with my hands all my life?" Jasim replied.

"Your crime this time is very serious. Will you be absolved, or will you be hanged?" said the prisoner.

Jasim snapped, "I will cry in court and ask to be hanged just to get rid of your questions and your mates."

The whole cell burst into laughter, yet this time Jasim was not angry and did not threaten to stop talking.

A Man for a Lonely Woman

Samia Dayyub tossed the book she was reading in a corner of her bedroom, turned off her bedside lamp, and put her head down, hoping to fall into a long, deep sleep. She couldn't sleep a wink, though. She was exasperated and disheartened because she was a beautiful, attractive, pretty, captivating, and cheerful woman. She was irresistible. She was cultivated, intelligent, and rich. She had inherited her wealth from her deceased father. She owned a car which aroused envy as well as an elegantly furnished and expensive house.

Still every time she met a man she liked, he looked to her like a little fish scared to get too close to a whale that might swallow him, and he disappeared like salt sprinkled on a sea.

Samia couldn't sleep, and by the time the sun rose, she was still staring at the ceiling mindlessly. She was torn apart with frustration, and she swore she would just accept the first man who proposed to marry her, even a dog scabbier than the strained dogs on the street.

Samia looked around and felt as if her house was shrinking and suffocating her. She thought that going for a walk outside and getting some fresh air might relieve her misery. No sooner had she left the house, though, she was surrounded by a bunch of dogs holding up their tails and noses. Every one of them barked, claiming he was the first one and the fittest to become her spouse.

Samia snapped at them, "You don't seem to have understood. You only paid attention to the first, sensible half of my oath. In fact, the second, reckless part of it is that on the first night of my marriage I will poison my husband's food and I will murder him for showing up so late in my life."

The dogs walked back and stopped barking. Samia asked them defiantly: "Who's still willing to marry me?"

The dogs fled and Samia roamed the streets with her head held high. She smelt the air mixed with petrol, dust, and the stink of rotten rubbish. She kept walking until she was tired and hungry, but she suddenly remembered that a friend she had known for five years had invited her for lunch, so she made her way to the restaurant and found him waiting for her. They ate lunch together, but Samia noticed her friend was shaking. "What's wrong?" she inquired. His face turned red, and he told her that he was going to ask from her something that he hoped would not anger her or make her stop seeing him again. Samia felt that the black flags fluttering on her existence were about to be hauled down and burned.

"Ask me anything you want, I won't be mad," she said to him. In a stuttering voice curbed by shame, he asked her to let him touch her hand, which made Samia lose her temper. "You dared to ask me to let you touch my hand after five years of friendship," she snarled at her friend. "Well, you will need fifty years to ask me to hold it and five hundred years to touch my knees."

She left the restaurant fuming, got on a bus and sat down. A fight broke out between the inspector and a young passenger, because the inspector didn't want to change a big bill the young passenger gave him to pay for the ticket. The inspector stopped the bus and asked the tall young passenger to leave, but he planted himself in his seat and refused to. Samia paid the inspector and the young man sat next to her. He thanked her profusely and almost excessively. She liked his eyes, the eyes of a man capable of murdering someone and, at the same time, those of a naïve joyful child. He had thick, black hair smooth as a horsetail and his face she could look at all day without getting tired of it. He was two or three years older than her. She gave him a cunning smile.

"Stop thanking me, you might end up asking me to marry you to express your gratitude," Samia said to him.

He surprised her as he immediately replied with eagerness: "If only you said yes!" Samia remembered the pledge she took in the morning and asked him, laughing: "And how would you ask me to marry you if we don't know each other?" He took her hand with great spontaneity, as if they were old friends and said to her: "I always said I would only marry a woman who makes me shiver when she looks at me and whose smile makes my fear vanish."

"I'm looking at you, are you scared?"

"I'm so scared I want to bury myself under the blanket."

"When do we get married?"

"Upon completion of the relevant procedures for marriage."

"When? In a year? In ten years?"

"I've never got married and I think my life will end in a few days."

"Either we get married today, or we don't get married."

"You do know about the housing crisis?"

"I have a big fancy house which can accommodate ten families."

The young man smiled, and his hand let go of hers. Her hand felt a strange desolation. The young man stood up getting ready to alight from the bus. "Why are you standing?" Samia asked him. "You look like you want to run away because you're scared."

"Let's just go to your house at once, there's no need to waste time."

As they approached her house, the young man asked her inquisitively: "How many beds does your house have?"

"One."

"That should do for the two of us and for a kid or two."

"My name is Samia, what's your name?"

"Tariq Ibn Ziad."

"Your real name."

"Tariq al-Mur'i and you will be Samia al-Mur'i."

"Where do you live?"

"With my parents in the Queiq neighborhood."

"I've never heard of that area before."

"God forbid! Although it's a well-known area, people who live in apartment blocks don't know about it."

"What do you do?"

"I've been unemployed for a year. I've been look-ing for a job but I haven't found anything."

Samia Dayyub smiled enigmatically. When they got to her house, she gave Tariq al-Mur'i a new job, but not exactly a very hard one. She woke up in the morning and was shocked to see her house looked bigger than she thought it was, big enough for tens of children to play and have fun in it. As they were having breakfast, she never stopped talking cheer-fully, while Tariq ate silently and running through the names of his friends from Queiq, scanning for the one who might be the right person for the flesh of this beautiful woman, for a substantial sum of course.

The Disgraced

Ghalib al-Halas is a disgraced man. His grandfather was murdered after he sold himself cheap to a foreign occupying army. His father looked like a skeleton covered in a yellow dangling skin. He would kill or even risk his own life to get into bed with maids. Any women whose body didn't smell of onion and garlic made him sick. The guy working at the butcher's had some unbelievable stories about Ghalib al-Halas's mother. He claimed that every time he went to deliver meat to her house, she grabbed him to lure him inside and wouldn't let him go until he turned into a flaccid chunk of meat with two legs unable to walk. His paternal aunt enjoyed stealing spoons from restaurants and bath towels from public baths. His maternal aunt's neighbors fled their homes and ended up sleeping on pavements to get away from her nosiness and gossip. His sister ran away from a mental institution where she was locked up because her insanity is contagious and can be transmitted through sight, hearing, and breath. His brother hunted stray dogs, slaughtered them, and sold their meat claiming it was fresh young lamb. His wife went after young pretty women. She was willing to pay whatever price they asked, and she bought expensive gifts to those who were too ashamed to name a price. His son, the muscular young man, whom men used to scramble to have his services, was now the one seeking them and paying them, begging for their approval. His daughter's husband divorced her because he was unable to satisfy her round-the-clock demands, and he returned her to her family. He told them she wasn't a woman, she was an oven in constant need of wood and they should marry her off to a hundred men.

The truth about Ghalib al-Halas was exposed. He was born out of wedlock to an unknown father, and everything he owned, such as money, property, and farms was amassed fraudulently. He didn't care about those scandals, he kept walking amongst people on a red carpet and his wealth kept on growing.

The Cat

Despite being fifty years old, Muti' al-Maqtu' had never got married. He was content living alone in a shabby little house with a white cat that he spoiled as if she were a child. He worked in a government agency and what he made wasn't enough for him to eat three meals a day, but he still cared for his cat. He worried when he was away from his cat and spent all his time with her after coming home from work. He didn't complain or protest, he was always merry, he laughed at his hardships and didn't worry about anything. He changed when his cat disappeared, though, and became grim, angry, and scowling. He went out of his way to look for his cat; he knocked on the door of every house in the neighborhood, begging for help. He even paid the kids in the neighborhood, hoping they would give him information as to the cat's whereabouts, all for nothing. He didn't find the cat, she was like a bird that had flown away. Had she died or been killed, he would have found her body, and had she been stolen, someone would have seen her. Had she drifted away from his house and got lost, she would have come back sooner or later because, after all, she was accustomed to leaving the house with him when he set off to work in the morning, roaming the neighborhood until he came home.

Muti' al-Maqtu' wanted to accuse his enemies of kidnapping his cat, except that he had no enemies at all. Some of his male neighbors reproached him for his endless misery at his cat's absence, to which he replied that his cat wasn't an ordinary cat. His cat could speak like a human being, and she was going to point him to the place in his house where a treasure was buried, and if she had not vanished, she would have made him rich. His words were met with hypocritical smiles and looks full of doubt about his mental soundness. People started saying that losing his cat made Muti' lose his mind as well, until one day, after months, the cat returned hungry, cold, and dirty. Muti' al-Maqtu' almost fainted with happiness. If he had a wife in his house, he would have had her shout zaghrutas in celebration. People went up to his house to congratulate him and he received them with a smile on his face, his ears all red as if he had just become a father. He borrowed money from the grocer and the butcher to organize a banquet in celebration of the cat's return. His luck seemed to have turned too, as he was unexpectedly appointed general director of an anti-smuggling section. He left his little house and bought a bigger, fancier one, and started eating five meals a day. Spinsters and divorcees in the neighborhood now vied to seduce him and rumor had it that the cat kept her promise and led him to hidden treasures.

A Cold Night

Abdallah al-Qasir stretched in his bedroom, listening to the raindrops tapping on the windowpane, as he got into his bed and sprawled on it. "Hurry up," he said to his wife Bahira.

Bahira turned off the bedside lamp and she laughed as she slipped under the blanket next to Abdallah. He hugged her and whispered to her: "It's so cold tonight."

They heard a female voice calling for help, which alarmed Bahira because she recognized it as the voice of their neighbor Wafiqa, who lived alone since her husband left. She was a lonely pretty woman, and perhaps she was shouting because a stranger broke into her bedroom to assault her. "We're not her only neighbors," said Abdallah, "someone else will help her."

"No one is going to help her," said Bahira. "They're all lazy, sleepy, and cold like you."

"I don't hear her anymore," said Abdallah.

"Maybe the intruder has shut her mouth," said Bahira, "and is already ripping her clothes."

"Go on," said Abdallah as he hugged her tighter, "tell me what else they're doing."

Bahira started telling him but her voice quavered, until he couldn't understand what she was saying. Meanwhile, the wind outside their room was blowing through empty dark roads.

The Silent

Zuhair Sabri met a woman who looked like a red flower on a green twig. She told him in a trembling voice that she loved him and she could never love any other man. He told her he only cared about his own future and, suddenly, a painful slap hit him on the nape of his neck, but as he turned around, he couldn't see who hit him.

Later, he was slapped a second time, when he called a wealthy man "the country's greatest man," but again he couldn't figure out who hit him.

He was slapped again a third time when he kissed the hand of a man with a long scruffy beard, pleading him to pray for his soul, and this time too he didn't know who hit him.

Zuhair Sabri was slapped again many times every day, unable to see who slapped him. He didn't talk to anybody about those unseen blows lest people would laugh at him or think he was crazy. He was positive, though, that all people got slapped just like him but they didn't say anything.

He Doesn't Know

Tarif al-Nabri was over an hour late to meet with his old friends at the bar where they habitually met. His mates greeted him with roars of excitement. He looked at the empty bottles on their table and said to them: "I can see that you didn't wait for me."

"Enough with that rubbish," said to him one of the three languidly. "Sit down and drink fast so you can come to your senses and we can understand each other."

Tarif nodded, happy to let the alcohol take effect and started drinking neat whisky, one glass after another, eager to make up for lost time and catch up with his friends. Once he was as drunk as the others, or perhaps more, he took out from his pocket a photograph of a woman who looked like a white carnation and, as the alcohol made him stutter, he swore he didn't know that woman and that he had never seen her in his life. He didn't know who gave him her picture and he didn't know that her name was Leila. He didn't know that her hair was black and her face was white. He didn't know that she had big green eyes. He didn't know that she worked every day in a trading company whose offices were on a street he was accustomed to roam. He didn't know that she lived in a small apartment which consisted of two tiny rooms. He didn't know her bed and that she liked silk pajamas and that her favorite color was blue. He didn't know that anger and joy both made her hair sweaty. He didn't know that she didn't like restaurant food and that she was a brilliant cook. He didn't know that she liked laughing, smoking cigarettes, petting cats, and walking at night. He didn't know that her unborn baby committed suicide too. He didn't know that she left a short letter written in bad handwriting and plenty of grammatical mistakes, with more love than reproach in it. He didn't know why she reproached him, he didn't know her and she didn't know him. And had she known him, he would have known she knew him and he wouldn't have said that he didn't know her.

The waiter asked Tarif if he wished to eat dinner. He replied saying he would leave it to his friends to decide and that he would have whatever they were going to have. The waiter laughed and Tarif realized that his friends had left him alone without him noticing. His hands clung to the photograph of a woman he didn't know, neither did he know that she loved him and that he loved her. Had he known, he wouldn't have denied it.

The Advisors

'Azmi al-Saffad used to spend most of his time in the neighborhood cemetery. He would reply firmly to those who mocked him by saying that every head is free to choose its own pillow. "What's best for me?" asked 'Azmi. "To sit in the cemetery or in a bar, or in a strip club or in a casino?"

His long hours sitting in the cemetery earned 'Azmi the trust, affection, and respect of the dead of which he only befriended the most prominent, because he believed that if you mingle with the poor, you get fleas.

He befriended Hamza al-Rakba, a bank director who died in prison after being convicted of embezzlement. The millions he stole were never recovered and he earned the respect of both the inmates and the wardens for the rest of his life.

He also befriended Rashid Nasr, who owned as many houses, businesses, and estates as hairs on his head. And he wasn't bald, he had a thick head of hair. He was a Don Juan, marrying and divorcing one woman after another, for there are as many women out there as there are grains of sand in the desert, and life is short, one has to be quick if he wants to right-fully get with all of them.

He befriended Karim al-Maqal, who held many important roles, the last one of which was minister of finance. During his term, a rumor spread about him being different from all the other people because his clothes had endless visible and invisible pockets, and even when his invisible pockets were too full, there were other empty pockets begging to be filled like the other lucky pockets. When he died of a sudden heart attack, flags were flown at half-mast and he was mourned as a martyr, a symbol of the country's econ-omy lost forever.

He befriended Nazeer al-Bahlul who, although he murdered and shed people's blood as if it were water, met his demise in a petty fight, making people remi-nisce the famous proverb that goes, "A mosquito can make the lion's eye bleed."

He befriended ʿAmid al-Helu, a famous writer, who circulated amongst notables and dignitaries a menu for his eulogies and satires whose prices were not negotiable. Every letter of the alphabet had a price, and the price of a ق, for example, wasn't like that of a ي. He died having never written a word for charity or out of altruism, as he would only write after having been paid. As long as they guaranteed that they would pay him, he promised that he would write. No more, no less.

He befriended Jalil al-ʿIath, who was trying to invent a new type of bomb, one that could decimate millions of people and make him rich. What Jalil was trying to invent burst, turning him into tiny chunks of flesh that could only be seen through a microscope.

He befriended Dalal al-'Addad, whose life was an endless chain of scandals. She was accused of luring respectable wives into selling their bodies, and of setting up a secret prostitution ring which included schoolgirls. She survived all accusations, kept her head held high and preserved her excellent reputation all the same. Her services remained popular and continued to enjoy marketability, appreciation, and respect. When she died, people's eyes filled with tears and her memory was treated with such respect and reverence as if she were Rabi'a al-'Adawia.

These seven friends volunteered to work as unpaid advisors for 'Azmi al-Saffad, which he accepted gladly. Their first advice to him was to stop sitting in the cemetery lest people thought he was eccentric and started spreading rumors about his mental stability. When he tried to retort and expound his loyalty to his friends, they told him that they would accompany him wherever he would go.

When 'Azmi al-Saffad entered public life, he could count on seven expert, experienced, mature, and smart advisors. He went from one success to the other and became his country's wealthiest and most influential man. His commands were swiftly followed, the first order being to prohibit people from sitting in cemeteries.

Sixty Years

Bashira complained to her doctor about a strange mix of fatigue, nausea, and headache. The doctor examined her forehead and told her that he would be able to diagnose her disease accurately and successfully only after taking some necessary tests, which he would have to send to a laboratory. Pending the required analyses, they scheduled a second appointment after several days.

In the second visit, the doctor browsed the medical report and said to her cheerfully:

"Congratulations! You are pregnant and your health is excellent."

"God bless you brother," Bashira replied to her doctor, "but cut the jokes please."

"I'm not kidding. You are pregnant in your third month," said the doctor firmly.

"That's impossible," said Bashira in shock. "How could I conceive? I'm sixty and I haven't been with a man since my husband died two years ago."

"What happened is strange, indeed, but the results of the test don't lie," the doctor told her.

"There must be a mistake . . ."

The doctor interrupted her: "There is no room for inaccuracies with reliable laboratories such as ours," he said sounding offended.

"What do I say to my sons and their wives, my daughters and their husbands, my relatives, acquaintances, and neighbors? Who is going to believe me?"

"The world is a holy mess," the doctor said. "You would feel sorry for me if I told you the things I have to deal with . . . Today I had a young couple whose tests revealed that the wife is pregnant and the husband has cancer. He won't live to witness his wife give birth."

Bashira went home half-crazy and wandered around her house, unable to figure out what to do when, suddenly, the fetus moved in her belly. She lay on her bed and put her palms on it and felt the fetus talking to her without having to resort to words or sounds. She felt that all the fetus wanted made its course through her veins to become what she desired and longed for. What the fetus wanted now was to escape scandals, gossip, and poisonous rumors. He wanted to fall asleep, astonished by her sixty years of patience. But she couldn't sleep and took all the sleeping pills she had and pain killers too.

I will be relieved of illness and its pain.

You will be free to run from a stupid doctor to a crazy doctor and from spending a lot of money on something useless.

I will rest from climbing the stairs to my house on the fourth floor.

You will be done with cleaning the house.

I will be done with cooking.

You will be done with chewing and swallowing food.

I will be done with talking to people.

You will be done with talking to yourself.

I will be done with loneliness and solitude.

You will be done with missing your daughters and sons that live in homes far from you and you just see at occasions.

When Bashira fell asleep, she imagined that she heard the fetus laugh at her scornfully. She tried to speak, but the fetus did not want to speak and forced her to close her eyes forever.

The Blonde!

Mahdi al-Qattam took off the black clothes he wore to mourn his departed wife, who died suddenly very young, and gave them to the first beggar who extended his hand to him. He remarried with a woman from another neighborhood, who was different from the women of his own. She had blue eyes, stark white skin, and blonde hair, which stirred a wave of gossip and rumors, until some of the neighborhood's men daringly confronted Mahdi al-Qattam in public for remarrying too soon without honoring the dead. Mahdi, showing disgust, said to the men reproachfully: "You ignorant fools! If you knew the blonde woman I married, you would not be giving me such stupid silly talk."

The men were speechless and dumbfounded. All the women they knew were brunettes or fair skinned with black hair. They had never met a blonde woman in all their lives, so they wondered among themselves: "Do blonde women have something that brunettes don't have?" There was no blonde woman in their neighborhood apart from Mahdi's wife, which became the only way for them to find out and, therefore, to increase their knowledge of women and to fill that shameful gap in their expertise.

However, Fouad al-Mujammer advised them not to waste their time because the blonde would soon give in and fall hopelessly in love with him. The men asked him curiously about his plan, but he refused to disclose it to them as he recalled that victory in love is not different from victory in war and anyone who discloses their plans is inevitably defeated. The men were confused as Fouad was not particularly handsome, rich, smart, educated, or erudite, nor had an eventful existence and, when he talked, he made whoever was listening yawn and fall asleep. His body was neither a man's nor a woman's, yet he spoke with great confidence about the future of his relationship with the blonde woman. There had to be some truth to it because there is no smoke without fire, as they say. So, they eagerly awaited, heedless of their wives dyeing their hair blonde and turning even more loathsome and hideous than they were.

Only a few days had passed when Fouad entered the café with his head wrapped in white bandages. He told the men gathered around him that the blonde wanted to caress him and express her love for him as he was passing by her house, so she threw from the upper window a heavy flowerpot full of dirt, gravel, and red roses that landed on his head. The result was a bloody head, which sent him to the nearest hospital crying for doctors and nurses to succor him. Jamil al-Satal laughed sarcastically and said to Fouad:

"We thought the pasha was indeed a pasha."

"What do you mean?" Fouad asked him nervously.

"I mean that the blonde would not love somebody like you."

"Do you mean that she will love somebody like you instead?"

"You will see . . . only time will tell."

The men awaited eagerly for what was going to happen next, wondering who would prevail, Jamil al-Satal or Fouad al-Mujammer?

Jamil al-Satal came to the café the next day. He could hardly walk and was groaning in pain. He sat on a chair and took off his shoes showing his red, swollen bleeding feet. He explained that he saw the blonde walking in the street and teased her with such politeness that she was ashamed to express to him her passion and reciprocate publicly in front of a crowd. She complained to a cop who happened to be passing by and who dragged Jamil to the police station where they threw him to the floor and beat with a stick on his soles until he cried his regret for what he had done. Sakhr Abbas asked him then:

"And the blonde? Did you forget her?"

"I did what I had to do," Jamil replied. "I was hitting on her and now I am waiting for her to answer me and tease me back. The ball is in her court now."

"What if she's shy and does not respond in kind . . ." Sakhr asked him. "Are we allowed to hit on her?"

Jamil addressed the whole group of men, looking at them in the eyes and asked them inquisitively: "Are you going to?"

Sakhr said to him: "God forbid, no! Do you think we are degenerate men like you with no respect for the honor of respectable women?"

One night, four masked men sneaked into Mahdi's house and found him sleeping on his bed next to his blonde wife. They tied him with ropes while he cried and begged them not to kill him. He pointed them to the place where he hid his money, even though they didn't ask him to. The four men moved toward his wife and she tried to fight them. The husband screamed at his wife, reproaching her for her poor manners. After all, these men were his guests and people should spare no pains in treating their guests hospitably. The blonde woman quickly took off her clothes and lay on the bed defiantly, which convinced the men that she was an inconsiderate hostess because she didn't say "please" or "be my guests." To them, she looked like a frog laying on its back floating on the surface of water, only bigger, yet their desire to increase their knowledge of women blinded them and rid them of any reluctance. They assaulted her all at once, elbowing each other loudly but, in the commotion, they tore off her blonde hair, which turned out to be nothing but a wig, while her real hair was black, short, coarse, and frizzy. That did nothing to put them off and they only left her after what felt, at the same time, a long and short while. They exchanged looks filled with disappointment and returned to their wives eagerly, as if they had been away in desolate, uninhabited deserts for years, but they couldn't say a single word to their neighbors about the fake blonde hair. Mahdi kept what happened to him, his money and his wife as a secret, and the blonde woman remained desirable, sought after and unattainable.

The Branches

Bilal al-Dandashi went to his school in the morning as usual. He got there late and entered the school quivering with fear toward his teacher and his insensitive and sarcastic reprimands. When he entered, he found the pupils and the teachers asleep, and he tried to wake them up but to no avail. He got weary of sitting alone, yawned, and fell asleep. He saw in his dream that he was asleep in a school whose students were all sleeping deeply, heedless to their teacher's angry yelling. His mother woke him up and urged him to hurry up lest he be late for school. Bilal dashed off, heading over to his school only to find that the teachers had been slain and the pupils were playing around cheerfully. He didn't play with them because his mother woke him up to send him to school. He put his clothes on hastily and set off with an empty stomach. He quickly made his way to school and sat in his class among the other pupils, preparing himself for what was about to happen. The teacher came in with a frown and a stern look in his eyes. The pupils stared at him with hatred and started exchanging unintelligible remarks until the teacher shouted furiously: "Quiet!"

The pupils went silent. The teacher put his shabby bag on the desk and opened it. He took out a pile of papers and waved them, saying to his pupils: "Do you know what these papers are? They are your answers to my question about the profession you want when you become men."

He approached the rubbish bin, waved the papers around once more and said: "These answers deserve less than zero." He threw the papers in the waste-paper basket as if they were a disgusting piece of garbage and said to his pupils: "I have taught you the national anthem for days so that you can sing it at the party for the end of the academic year. Today I will test your memorizing skills and they better be good."

The kids whispered and grumbled to each other. "Quiet!" the teacher yelled again fuming.

The pupils went quiet, and their teacher said to them: "I will count to three and when I say three, you start singing the national anthem together. Ready? One . . . two . . . three."

The pupils exchanged cryptic glances and started singing loudly the lyrics from a popular love song on the melody of the national anthem. The teacher bellowed: "Quiet!"

The pupils darted toward the teacher like a speeding bullet and hit him with their rulers, their books, their notebooks, and kicked him with their feet, telling him to shut up. The teacher was shocked at what was happening and yelled frantically, asking for help, but nobody came. He tottered and collapsed to the ground as his legs had just been hit by a series of painful blows. He tried to hold his ground, intimidate, threaten, or just to endure it, but an insufferable pain compelled him to cry and beg the children to stop beating him. The pupils didn't put an end to their beating until the teacher gave in and fell silent. The children tied him with a rope they had found and ordered him to sing the national anthem. The teacher obeyed and, with a rattle in his throat which made his voice quiver, he started reciting the national anthem. The pupils put their hands on their ears in disgust. Bilal al-Dandashi emerged from the group of children and stood before them, imitating their teacher's posture. He shouted in a cheerful commanding voice: "One . . . two . . . three."

The pupils' voice rose reciting the national anthem in perfect harmony and coordination. Their voices became one and left through the window and surged into waves.

Another House

Khalid al-Hallab seemed to have forgotten that he had stood humiliated in front of a stern judge who decreed his eviction from the house he had lived in since he was a child and, after the midday prayer, he listened obediently and in delight to someone who said that heaven lies under the feet of mothers. He went home, picked up a shovel and a pickaxe and started digging the ground under his mother, who had been sitting on a wooden chair in the courtyard and wouldn't stop moaning in pain. He went on digging for hours and came across nothing but earth and damp. He hurled the shovel and the pickaxe in anger and helped his mother to sip her mix of tea, extra sugar, and crushed sleeping pills. She fell asleep shortly after and he proceeded to place two pillows at the bottom of the dig; he carried his mother and laid her out on a shroud. He then sat on her chair, tired and out of breath. He drank up the rest of his mother's tea and stretched out in the hole next to her. He clutched her cold hand and closed his eyes, hoping the night would come soon when it would be time to shovel soil into the pit.

The Enterprise

Shahira was walking in her neighborhood with a frown on her face, while her husband Mustafa was trying to keep up with her, moaning about her unnecessary speed. No sooner had they entered the house than she started yelling at him furiously:

"I want a divorce, now!"

"What happened?" Mustafa replied in astonishment. "What's up?"

"Don't pretend that I didn't catch you with my sister," said Shahira. "Ugh, you were like animals. Is that what you call private tutoring in chemistry and maths?"

"I am innocent," said Mustafa. "Your sister is the one who started it and I didn't even try to dissuade her, because humiliating a young girl in her early youth is one of the biggest pedagogical mistakes that can cause a series of endless psychological issues. Isn't it time for you to change? You've always been selfish, you only think of yourself but never about your sister and her future."

Shahira was confused and went silent, she looked like she was thinking. Suddenly, she said to Mustafa:

"Don't lie and tell me the truth. Who's the cutest . . . me or my sister?"

"What kind of stupid question is this?" said Mustafa. "You cannot compare the sky and the earth. Your sister thinks she's as graceful as a gazelle, she doesn't realize she has more bones than flesh and, as you know, I hate bones and I am all about flesh."

Shahira smiled, stretched, and said to Mustafa: "I don't believe you."

"Wait a little until the fear you felt when you caught me giving chemistry and math lessons to your sister vanishes," said Mustafa.

Shahira waited patiently, but she got even madder when, a few days later, she caught him cheating on her with their maid. She kicked the maid out of the house threatening her:

"I will break your legs if you come anywhere near this house again."

"Had she been a pretty young girl," she yelled at Mustafa, "I would have excused you, but she's hideous and older than my mother."

"When one is forced to eat baklava all the time," said Mustafa, "he will develop a craving for falafel."

"Are you saying I am baklava and the maid is falafel?" Shahira asked him.

"God forbid! She's less than falafel," Mustafa replied.

"And yet I caught you devouring that falafel as if you hadn't eaten for a thousand years."

"Do you want me to swear that I have repented and that I will never eat falafel until the day I die?"

"I want you to swear that you will never cheat on me again."

"I won't swear, because every year I need to cheat on you at least once to realize how much I love you."

Shahira looked at him, struggling to believe what she had just heard. He said to her confidently: "Every time I sleep with another woman, I realize you're the only woman I love, a feeling that I can only get by having an affair."

Shahira asked him "Are you trying to convince me that you cheat on me because you love me?"

"Could you rephrase that please? The right wording for it is that I cheat on you in order to find out how much I love you. Someone tall can only realize they're tall by standing amongst short people."

"Do you think I'm that stupid, to believe your nonsense?"

"Don't be unfair. You're not stupid and this is not nonsense."

"You're only saying you love me, but you don't mean it."

He swore to her that the falafel had ruined his mood, his appetite, and his stomach. He needed some time to sort himself out and Shahira waited for him patiently for a long time.

One day, Mustafa noticed that Shahira had changed and that she had started cheating on him with young men that she chose carefully. He swooped down on her like a mean cat on a little mouse. He confronted her with the facts, making her blush. She didn't deny it and replied that she felt sorry for those boys, because failure in their early age could compromise their future and they needed someone to teach them and provide guidance. He later caught her having affairs with men from a wide range of professions and backgrounds as if she were a researcher compiling an extensive study on the secrets of an uncharted society. She glanced at him rebukingly and swore that she had done what she had only to test her love for him. She asked him, "If I knew you and no other man apart from you, how could I know that you're the best and that I'm not being deceived?"

Mustafa didn't dare to divorce her because her father was wealthy and generous. They carried on living together as husband and wife, both with their daily attempts to prove their love to each another.

The Thickets

A heated bout of that card game called conquian was taking place in the café between Ma'rouf al-Samma' and Rashid al-Qalil, while a group of men watched, cheered, and threw sarcastic comments at them. The game ended with Rashid's defeat and Ma'rouf boasting about his victory. The latter suggested to his opponent that he continue practicing day and night before playing against an ace like him, which made Rashid lose his temper, rip up the cards, and throw them to the ground. In a loud voice that all the café's customers could hear, Rashid told Ma'rouf to cut down the bragging in front of men who knew his sister's body more than her own mother. Ma'rouf lowered his head and didn't say a word. He heard whispering voices only he could hear.

The rabbit whispered, "Run for your life."

The ostrich whispered, "Burying your head today will lead to burying your entire body tomorrow."

The hyena whispered, "He who doesn't eat, gets eaten."

The snake whispered, "My skin is soft and death lies in my fangs."

The wolf whispered, "If you weren't a wolf, the sheep would eat you."

The raven whispered, "I miss croaking so much!"

The lion didn't say anything, he just gave out an angry roar preparing to fall on his prey. Ma'rouf sprang up from his chair as though he wanted to leave the café and slapped Rashid twice on his right and left cheek. Rashid was amazed and astonished because he was expecting an exchange of insults, followed by a brawl, followed by the other men breaking them up, but Ma'rouf took out a knife promptly and stabbed Rashid in his chest three times.

"Ouch, you killed me!" Rashid bellowed.

The lion moved away from his prey, blood still dripping from his mouth. Ma'rouf ran away from the café still holding his blood-dripping knife and, as he was running, he realized that he was an only child and that he didn't have a sister.

The Lying Hand

Muwaffaq al-Nims liked to paint the outside of his house every summer with a limpid white paint. He was shocked when, one day, a nameless hand wrote on his house wall with black paint and in capital letters, questioning his wife's loyalty to him. This made Muwaffaq blow up and he set off immediately to get some yellow paint with which he wrote—below what the nameless hand had written and in even bigger letters—that his wife was the most virtuous woman on the face of the earth. The nameless hand replied claiming that his ugly wife did as she pleased while he was at work and he had no idea what was going on. These absurdities offended Muwaffaq, who replied by writing that, while he was at work, his pretty wife was busy cleaning the house, cooking, and waiting on tenterhooks for him to come home. The nameless hand retorted that red was his wife's favorite underwear color. Muwaffaq laughed at the nameless hand's imbecility and wrote on his wall in yellow paint and in even bigger letters that black was his wife's favorite underwear color, which caused the nameless hand to remain silent and unable to reply.

The Testimony

Bahiya boasted to the other women about how she preserved her honor and the honor of the neighborhood where she was born. She recounted what happened to her the day before, while she was walking in an orchard nearby. The unknown man who raped her took out a knife so big it could have taken out a camel and ordered her to remove all her clothes, threatening to kill her if she refused. She took off her clothes but left her socks on in defiance of the man and his knife. The women were impressed and from then on they strolled in the orchards determined not to remove their socks.

Eight O'Clock

At noon, Hanan al-Mulqi was walking fast on the street, indifferent to the glances of men dazzled by her beauty. She grunted her frustration at some young men harassing her, describing her as an untamed filly. When she got to the public park, she quickly went in, sat down on a bench, and sighed with relief. A twenty-five-year-old man came and sat next to her, smiling, and told her that he had walked around the park for more than ten times looking for her. They talked about the extreme heat, television series, roses in the garden, and ducks swimming in a large pond of blue water. He suddenly told her that he loved her and had loved her since the first time he laid eyes on her. She looked down with her chin upon her chest, her face turned red and yellow, and her hands shaking. He told her he wished to marry her if she agreed and implored her to break her silence and say something. She was upset and told him that she couldn't marry because she devoted her life to serve her sick parents who had nobody else in the world to take care of them. She looked at her wristwatch, stood up, terrified, and said to him that in a few minutes she had to be home to give her mother the medicine. They left the park together and Hanan waved at a taxi. The young man was keen to set the day for their next date. Hanan hesitated but then accepted to meet him again in five days. She got into the cab and told the driver the address while looking anxiously at her wristwatch.

When the car arrived at the address, she paid the driver, got out of the car, and went into a building. She walked up the stairs to the second floor and, at ten past one, she pressed the doorbell of one of the apartments. The door opened promptly as if somebody had been waiting behind it. A thirty-year-old man appeared, told her that she was late and that he thought she wasn't coming. She didn't answer him, went straight into the house, and proceeded to take off her clothes before he had even finished closing the door. At ten to two, she dressed in a hurry and told the man that she had to be home at two o'clock before her jealous husband came back from work and she made her way hastily.

At seven past two, Hanan entered a café frequented by men and women where she met a young man who was several years older than her. The man grabbed her hand, looked at her, clearly infatuated, and talked to her for half an hour about what he wished to become after graduating from college. She listened to him with interest and respect and told him that she had to leave because she had an appointment with a doctor. The man asked her what the issue was, and she told him that the initial diagnosis had indicated that she had cancer and she might not have long to live.

At three o'clock, Hanan met a fifty-year-old man and they went into the cinema together. The lights went off and the film started. The man tried to hold her hand, but she got up and left the cinema angrily. The man followed her and tried to apologize. She said to him: "Who do you think you are? How dare you hold my hand?"

The man said that he was very sorry, but she didn't accept his apology. He then told her that he wasn't married because he had never met a woman with such morals. She told him that she was a nurse and she was late for work at the hospital. She was so upset when she left him, she was shaking.

At five o'clock, Hanan entered a women's clothing store. She chose a yellow dress and tried it on in front of a mirror in the dressing room. She called the shop's manager and asked him for assistance. His assistance went on for quite a long time, making them both sweat profusely. She left the shop without buying the dress because she didn't like it.

At six o'clock, Hanan went to a restaurant where a sixty-year-old man was waiting for her. They ate their food silently until the old man suddenly said to her, staring at her lips: "You are always pretty, but today you are even prettier. I wish I had a million dollars to pay you for one fraternal kiss."

Hanan answered him, "A kiss is always free because I consider it to be simply publicity, as well as a form of zakat or charity. As for more than just a kiss, even the richest men cannot afford to pay for it."

"I am poor and miserable, I'm content with what I get for free," the old man replied.

"I feel sorry for you, people like you should be given everything for free," said Hanan to him.

The old man said, "When and where?"

"Now and here, the sooner the better."

"What about the other people?" exclaimed the old man.

Hanan said, "What about on the stairs of a nearby building."

The old man asked her, "And what will we say if somebody catches us?"

"I will lie and say that you are my father," Hanan replied.

At seven o'clock in the evening, Hanan entered a dentist's clinic at a hurried pace and asked the secretary to see the doctor immediately because her toothache was killing her. The secretary looked anxiously at those who had been sitting waiting for their turn. She asked her quietly to wait for a little bit and then she let her into the dentist's room. Hanan sat on the chair and the doctor proceeded to examine her. She closed her eyes, but she did not open her mouth. When she came out of the dentist's room, she paid the prescribed fare and blushed thanking the secretary for helping her to get rid of the excruciating pain.

At half past seven, Hanan visited one of her friends. She told her she was annoyed because she had nothing to do with her life. Her friend concurred and went on and on about how bad boredom is.

At eight o'clock, Hanan returned to her house. Her father greeted her with a stern look on his face and asked her: "Where have you been? Why are you thirty minutes late?"

The mother rushed to intrude and said to the father reproachfully: "Pff! Don't you see that the girl is exhausted from all the studying she has done at university all day?"

Hanan was tired and went straight into her room, but her father said to her mother: "Thankfully God gave us a diligent daughter who loves to study." The mother agreed with him, and thanked God humbly.

The Ruins

The hammer was complaining to the anvil upon which it had been placed, until the latter said: "Shut up, relax and rest."

The hammer said, "I will not shut up because I am so sick of this life and of this shop that I want it demolished."

The anvil answered back, "What you feel and what you want is part of your rights, and no one is stopping you from exercising them except your laziness."

When Abdelmajid, the blacksmith, came to his workshop the next morning, he was shocked to find it all in shambles except for the hammer and the anvil. He was on the verge of tears. Upset and disheartened he sat down on a short wooden chair, disturbed at the whole scene.

The hammer then said to the anvil, "I am tired of this fool of a blacksmith who never tires of his work but gets poorer and poorer every day."

"Leave this blacksmith alone. He hasn't threatened our rights," the anvil replied.

The hammer and the anvil were tarnished with the blacksmith's blood. The anvil condemned the whole incident and confirmed to the police that its role was only that of the spectator. However, they ignored its statement and they did not arrest the killer.

A Beautiful Woman

Layla, whose surname was unknown, was a beautiful divorced woman. The director of the company she worked for raped her, and the taxi driver who took her to the police station raped her; the policeman who listened to her story raped her, and the doctor who examined her in order to make sure that the rape wasn't just a false claim raped her. The judge to whom she told in detail how she got raped three times also raped her, but he didn't rape her in court; he raped her in his office after asking her a few questions that couldn't be asked publicly. A journalist raped her, after he had noted everything she told him. Layla felt that the humiliation that she had endured required revenge and related what had happened to her to the Death. Death didn't rape her, it only flooded her flesh with ice that froze the blood in her veins.

The Mute

Walid Taymour left the dentist's clinic with numb
lips, gums, and tongue. He was walking on the pavement of a street hastily when the pavement asked him
sarcastically: "Are you training to take part in a race
or are you late for a date with a pretty woman?"

Then, one of the trees in the street said to him, "If
you rested on me for a while, my leaves would turn
yellow, dry out, and fall."

Walid ignored that and kept walking at the same
rapid pace. He passed by a black car that was parked
alongside the pavement, and the car said to him:
"Good morning."

Walid didn't answer that strange greeting addressed to him after sunset. He pulled out from his
pocket a pen and a piece of paper to write down the
car's plate number. Then the pen said to him: "You are
frowning for no reason, everything is perfectly fine."

As Walid tried to wipe his mouth, the handker-
chief said to him: "Don't be so nervous, your fingers
are shaking as if you were going to be hanged shortly
in an empty public square."

Walid ran out of patience and looked up to the sky, pretending to be turning to it for help, but the sky appeared to him as a huge black belly stabbed by a knife, ripping it apart from east to west. Snow-white cotton which turned into water when people touched it was raining down, except when Walid touched it nothing happened. He picked up enough cotton for a pillow, which he tried at midnight. No sooner had he put his head on it, that he heard the roar of sea waves mixed with the distant singing of children and women. He closed his eyes and slept peacefully for a very long time. He saw in his sleep people being tortured silently surrounded by chatter all around them.

The Rug Thieves

The police got their hands on a gang of thieves, consisting of three brothers, the oldest of which was ten years old. They confessed that they intended to steal the local mosque's carpets to lay them in their room. Their lies were quickly exposed, though, when the police searched their house and found out that their rooms were tiny and narrow, with enough space for just one little bed, whereas the size of the mosque's carpets was enough to furnish an entire palace. Under police interrogation the children disclosed their whole plan: they intended to dig up graves, uproot trees, smear black paint on the walls of white houses, spread rubbish all over the streets of their neighborhood, steal women's underwear, burn down all the houses, including theirs, and watch them turn into ashes with joy and satisfaction. Their father was very upset when he found out. He disapproved and disowned them, but in front of their mother he was proud of them and his eyes filled with tears.

Heaven

Hasan Jubran was told to pray ten times a day. He immediately obeyed and prayed eleven times every day despite his weak condition required rest and sleep.

Hasan Jubran was told to fast two months every year, so he fasted two months and nine days despite being weak and skinny.

Hasan Jubran was told to vote for the most stupid man to represent him and speak for him, and he quickly went to perform his duty proudly and happily.

Hasan Jubran was told to obey the authorities. He obeyed them and their servants to the extent that they convinced themselves that they were Gods.

Hasan Jubran was told to donate all he had to the poor. He obeyed and walked the streets naked, indifferent to the cries of derision and disapproval.

When he turned sixty-five, Hasan Jubran was rewarded with the exemption from prayers, fasting, and voting, and he was transferred to the desert where he became a camel chased around by female camels.

A Man Calling for Help

Fadwa Ibrahim heard the voice of a man calling her name as if he was asking her to help him. This didn't happen in her sleep or in a dream. When she heard this voice, she was at one of her friends', listening to her whining about her fiancé and his stupidity and recklessness. Her friend didn't seem to hear what Fadwa heard.

Fadwa was surprised that someone would think she could be able to help them. She heard the man's voice echoing her name again, as she was combing her grandmother's hair, and a third time, as she was walking in a public park. Then, while her mother was warning her not to waste her time with deceitful men, she heard the man's voice a fourth time. Many a night she woke up to that man echoing her name as if it were the only name he knew in the world.

Fadwa got used to the man calling for help and even cherished him. His calls didn't bother her, and she didn't tell anybody about him. She was secretly delighted at him, which put a mysterious smile on her face, making her feel she was venturing into a forest full of hidden dangers, intimately pervaded with a feeling of certainty that she would make it out of it alive.

Fadwa looked forward to meeting that man one day. She didn't regret it much when she no longer heard his voice after getting married. She thought that he had stopped calling for her help because he gave up or found someone who would help him and wouldn't neglect him for years.

One night, as they were getting ready for bed, Fadwa told her husband Ahmad with a reprimanding voice: "Did you notice that you did not talk to me for the whole evening, you didn't utter a single word but remained glued to the TV?"

Ahmad replied, "How can I talk to you when I am dead tired? Did you forget that I set off to work before sunrise this morning?"

"Tell me, how many years have passed since we got married?" Fadwa asked him.

Ahmad said, "Seven years, four months, and ten days."

"Every year you remember the day we got married and you bring me a gift," said Fadwa.

"I do not have a strong memory, but everything that has to do with you and our marriage, that I cannot forget," Ahmad replied.

Fadwa closed her eyes and said to Ahmad: "As long as you claim that your strong memory does not forget, tell me what's the color of my eyes?"

Ahmad thought for a very long time and then, exasperated, asked Fadwa to open her eyes, so he could tell her the color of her eyes.

Fadwa opened her eyes widely and said to Ahmad defiantly: "Come on, see for yourself and tell me."

Ahmad grumbled and kept staring at the television screen: "God damn this TV . . . all the programs tonight are so boring, a torture to watch."

Fadwa laughed and said to Ahmad sarcastically: "All you have to do is ask me to sing and dance for you and I will."

"No, no . . . *God does not impose on us a burden we cannot carry*," Ahmad replied. "But if you want to entertain me, there are other ways."

Fadwa, stretching, said to Ahmad: "I'd be happy if you named one."

"Why don't you tell me one of the stories you tell our son at night before bed?" said Ahmad.

Fadwa, upset by his request, told him in a tone that couldn't conceal her disappointment: "What pleases the young might not please the old."

Ahmad said to Fadwa: "You have a talent for making up excuses to escape, do not try to slip away from me."

"It's your fault. I will tell you a story that I haven't told our son because he is too young," Fadwa said to him.

"Tell me and I will definitely like the story as long as it doesn't suit children," Ahmad replied.

Fadwa licked her upper lip with her tongue and started:

"A long time ago, a king married a queen who used to tell him a story to amuse him every night. One night the queen remained silent.

The king asked her to tell him a story, but the queen said to him: "I've only one tale left, the story of the apple, can I tell it to you?"

The king replied: "Go on, tell the story! I love apples and everything that looks like apples."

The queen said: "I will tell you the story of the apple whether you love apples or hate them." The king, angry and astonished, looked at the queen, and she said to him: "I will tell you the story of the apple whether you are angry or happy. I will tell you the story whether you close your eyes or open them. I will tell you the apple's story whether you put your hands on your ears or not and I will tell you the story whether you smile or frown . . ."

"And what is the story of this apple?" Ahmad bellowed.

"Whether you ask about the story of the apple or not," Fadwa said. "I will tell you the story of the apple."

Ahmad threatened her: "If you don't tell me the story of the apple immediately, I will leave the house right now and go spend the evening at the nightclub."

"I will tell you the story of the apple," Fadwa replied, "whether you spend the evening at the night-club or the mosque."

Impatiently, Ahmad said to her: "Come on, tell the story. No more teasing."

"I will tell you the story of the apple, whether you ask for it or not, and I will tell you the story whether you are wearing your clothes or not."

Fadwa saw her husband getting dressed in frustration. He left the house angry, unable to hear the story of the apple. She waited for him to come home but he didn't. She went to sleep sad and in a dream she saw herself as a little schoolgirl getting beaten by her classmates. Then, she went home crying and her mother hugged her. Her mother promised to revenge her and beat her classmates, she patted her back at length until she stopped crying. She had another dream where naked men hit one another unlimitedly, letting out wild roars, their bodies smeared with blood. Terrified, she closed her eyes and waited for a man to wake her up, a man who could turn her on and inflame her with no more than a look, the same man who used to call her name, crying for help, a man she could touch with insatiable fingers and discover that he was less than a woman.

The Runaway

Najat al-Harabi ran away from her family's house and left her old grandmother a letter explaining the reasons for her escape. She said she had run out of patience and she could no longer tolerate more injustice. Her father beat her constantly; her mother confined her at home and forced her to clean day and night, and her brothers pestered her tirelessly. When the grandmother read the letter, she was astonished, amazed, confused, and depressed at the same time. Her granddaughter didn't have any siblings and her parents died when she was still a toddler. Najat always wished she had a rude, rough father; a very strict mother who would shout and whine all the time, and tough, cheerful, fickle brothers who could not tell an empty cloud from a rainy one.

The Oriental Dance

Razan al-Sukkari stood in front of the tall mirror in her room, her black hair loosely scattered on her shoulders. She started dancing to the notes coming out of the radio, imitating the style of professional dancers. The walls around her lost their dignified bearing and sighed deeply in admiration for that young, beautiful body, wishing they weren't made of cement. As she was dancing, Razan looked at the mirror, but instead of black hair and a white girl in the prime of life, she saw her father's disapproving, annoyed, disgusted look. She stopped dancing and ran to the living room where she found her father immersed in an old book. She looked at him dumb-founded, amazed at his capacity to be present in two places at the same time. Her amazement grew, along with her sadness, the day her brother hanged himself just before turning ten. Her father decided to keep the rope and swore in a suffocating voice that he would use it to hang whoever caused his son's demise. He kept his word and died hanged by the same rope.

The Surprise

The doctors told Nouraddin al-Tahhan that he had contracted an incurable disease and he didn't have more than six months to live. He received the news as if it were someone else whom he didn't know the one who got the disease. In the months that he had left to live—he said coldly—he would do everything he had dreamed of his whole life but had not dared doing. His family and friends expected months of exciting surprises from him but, instead, he carried on with his life as usual: he didn't sell or change his house, nor did he divorce his wife and free himself from her vile tongue; he didn't resign from his job, throwing the resignation letter with disdain to his boss, who enjoyed coming up with ways to humiliate him; nor did he squander the money he had inherited from his father. Instead, he carried on with his normal life until he died after nine years, two months, and three days.

Lo! The Horse Is Flying

A man took a woman to a field where there were only trees, grass, and a lean black horse grazing, and said to her: "Here no one will see us." He pulled her close to him and his mouth tried to eat her lips. She felt scared and her flesh asked for another kind of flesh, one that was tough, hot, rough, wet with copious sweat. She pushed the man away aggressively and asked him to stop pestering her. The woman pointed to the skinny horse who was pasturing in the field and told the man in a sarcastic tone that she might agree to marry him if that horse flew. The man was taken aback and looked at the horse with frustration.

"Look at the horse," he said to the woman in astonishment. "It looks like he is preparing to take off. Look at him . . . lo, he is flying!"

The woman looked and saw the horse arise. The horse started flying. She lay on the grass and saw the black horse hovering over in the blue sky. She sighed with relief, feeling comfortable and at ease. She clasped the man's waist as her arms were overwhelmed by a sudden force.

Modesty

Afaf knew she was pretty. Men loved her but women didn't. To women, she combined the qualities of a biting snake and a strutting peacock, and they dreaded her. She also knew that all of her co-workers, who pretended to be her friends, hated her and wished the worst for her after her relationship with the government minister was revealed, the news of which spread, making it the favorite subject gossipers whispered about.

Afaf wasn't annoyed by the news, the minister was a handsome man: good looking, sexy, generous, of sophisticated manners, and he mastered the art of sweet talking to women. He was influential, powerful, prestigious, respectful, and respected wherever he went. But, at the same time, she was afraid that the news would reach the ears of her husband Afif, who was tough, arrogant, stubborn, aggressive, and hostile. He wouldn't hesitate to divorce her, insult her in the most terrible ways, and destroy everything she had built throughout the years. In the best-case scenario, the least he would be content with would be that she quit her job and stay in the house like a slave.

Afaf tried her best to prepare herself for that grey day, thinking of every day that passed as a step toward a deep, bottomless pit. What she had anticipated and dreaded eventually did happen, as she was having lunch with her husband one day and she noticed that he kept looking at her. His looks were a mixture of blame, hostility, violence, and reproach, but she tried to ignore them. He kept staring at her in the same way until she couldn't help asking him: "What's wrong with you? You are you looking at me as if you were seeing me for the first time."

"Indeed, I am" said Afif to her.

Afaf replied, "You are looking at me as if I committed a sin."

"God forbid!" Afif said sarcastically. "You are an angel, all you need is a pair of wings."

Afaf looked down. Her heart was pounding as she asked him: "What do you mean?"

Afif raised his voice to reprimand her: "Did you forget the bread and salt that was between us? How could you forget ten years so quickly? Are you not ashamed that I am the last one to find out about you being the minister's favorite, and about him doing anything you want?"

She could barely speak and felt her blood was about to freeze in her veins: "They are just rumors," she said. "Don't believe any of it."

"I know you and I know you like to get away from anything you don't like," Afif retorted. "Why don't you just admit that you don't want to serve your poor husband anymore?"

Afaf was astonished, "What services are you talking about?"

"I have been waiting for months now for my application to the Ministry of Economy to go through and your minister is the Minister of Economy's best friend," Afif said. "One word from him would get the wheels in motion."

Afaf promised that she would talk to her minister the day after, and she would do anything she could to resolve the issue. "I have something very similar with the Minister of Supply too, but your minister is not his friend." Afif added, "Would you care to try and rub elbows with the Minister of Supply or his friend, the Minister of Interior?"

Afaf promised she would try to get to know all the ministers the same way she knew her own minister. Afif smiled and resumed eating his food voraciously, heaping praise on the person who made it.

The Beast

Huda rang her friend Nazik, who lived near her, and urged her to go to her house immediately because she could no longer stand her husband and his unbearable behavior. Nazik told her to stay calm and promised she would get there immediately. Nazik kept her promise and minutes later, as she sat in Huda's living room, she said: "Go on, tell me what happened today between you and your husband."

"Well, there is nothing new," said Huda. "It's just that I've had enough of this gloomy life and I am seriously thinking about divorce."

"No no, Huda. Anything but not a divorce," Nazik replied.

"I have been patient, I thought that he would change and come to his senses, but he hasn't changed a bit."

"Appearances can indeed be deceiving, but I always thought he was just a good-looking, polite, and well-behaved husband."

Huda disapproved. "Which politeness are you talking about? The same one you call polite and well-mannered is a capricious man, and anything female, even a fly, makes him drool. And if by accident a woman smiles at him, he thinks she is in love and dying to jump into bed with him."

Huda noticed that her friend had a sly smile on her face, "I know you and I know that smile," she asked her. "What is it?"

"Honestly, Huda," Nazik said to her, "when a man leaves his house sexually satiated, he doesn't even have the energy to spit on another woman, even the most attractive."

"And honestly, Nazik . . . All this beast can think of is getting into bed twenty-four hours a day. He has wild needs and I can't take it anymore."

"Thankfully God gave me a sweet and kind husband," said Nazik. "He wouldn't touch me without submitting a request a few weeks in advance and unless I give him my approval in writing."

Nazik gave her a long lecture about deprecating men like Huda's husband, explaining their behavior as the product of major personality weaknesses. Secretly, though, she was developing a fondness for that beast. She hoped to get a chance to smile at him, the smile of someone about to die unless she were kidnapped and raped by him.

The Laughing Woman Hired
as a Mourner

At the age of thirty, Shalabiyya was still single. She didn't marry any of her neighbors who were fascinated by her and dreamed of owning this mysterious, attractive, strong, and cheerful woman. She preferred to live alone and work in a profession she mastered. People paid her handsomely for singing, dancing, and shouting zaghrutas at weddings, as well as for crying and wailing at funerals. She was unrivalled. Without her, weddings were joyless and grim; and unless she was there at funerals, the family and friends of the deceased remained tearless.

One day, she was invited to a funeral at Sameh al-'Awam's house in exchange for an agreed and bargained fee. She sang, danced, and shouted zaghrutas of celebration and told whimsical stories that made the dead laugh. The family of the deceased were outraged. They showed her to the door and refused to pay her fee. On the same night, she attended a wedding in the house of Fouad al-Lamam and when she cried, whined, wailed, slapped her cheeks, and was about to tear her dress apart, she was again forced to leave the wedding without being given the fixed fare. The news of what Shalabiyya had done spread in Queiq and was met with such disapproval that people stopped hiring her for weddings and funerals. Shalabiyya never tried to defend herself or to explain what had happened. She decided to admit that she could no longer tell the difference between a funeral and a wedding. She unexpectedly started spending a lot more time on the prayer rug and became famous for a new, unknown supernatural ability which was greatly sought after. Those who couldn't overcome their stronger opponents would resort to her secret powers and her capacity to make their adversary drown in a sea of insurmountable misery.

One day, an old man, worn out by grief and sorrow, visited her secretly and told her that he was Najib al-Baqqar himself, a very well-known, wealthy, and respected man in her neighborhood. He was hoping she would agree to help him get back at his wife, as she was devoted to come up with new ways to humiliate him and insult him on a daily basis. She asked him inquisitively: "Why don't you divorce her and be done with it?"

He told her that, in order to avoid legal issues, he had had to register his huge fortune under his wife's name, whom he trusted blindly. However, she had suddenly changed and, from being like a meowing cat, she had turned into a howling wolf who treated him like a useless banana peel, tyrannizing him in order to force him to divorce her.

"Your wife deserves to die, torturing her would not be enough," said Shalabiyya.

Najib al-Baqqar looked at her in astonishment and exclaimed: "Subhan Allah for your words of wisdom! My wife does indeed deserve to die because, if she does, my wealth goes back under my name and I will be relieved."

Shalabiyya asked him in a cold, cautious tone: "What would you be willing to give for her death?"

Najib al-Baqqar answered right away: "I would give anything."

"All I want is for you to pay me a fair recompense every month for the rest of my life, enough so that I don't have to leave my house and deal with cheap scummy people. As for your wife, I will pray and plead for her to die of a sudden natural death in a few days," replied Shalabiyya.

A few days later, Najib al-Baqqar came to Shalabiyya in mourning clothes and tried to kiss her hands in gratitude and appreciation. Shalabiyya was embarrassed and she just muttered that she only helped those in need. However, she later found out that he had tricked her. His wife was a delicate, meek woman who was scared of her own shadow and would cry if she saw a bird freezing. He cunningly planned to get rid of her to put his hands on the houses, shops, and farms she inherited from her parents. What Najib al-Baqqar did made Shalabiyya livid with anger. She dismissed every visitor and spent the next days without eating nor speaking. Then, she returned to her old occupation of whining at weddings and singing zaghrutas at funerals uninvited. She didn't ask for any fee nor cared about children following her and making fun of her wherever she went in the neighborhood.

The Recompense

Nassouh al-Fani walked along the street at a slow pace that commanded reverence and veneration. People were rushing to him, competing to kiss his hand in token of submission. His voice quivered as he muttered to them that he wished for everyone to have success, great fortune, and good posterity. When he arrived at home, he found his wife, Hasiba, busy reading a women's magazine with a disgusted frown on her face, as if garbage had just been scattered all around her. She didn't even look at him or welcome him with a greeting. He secretly cursed the day he married a pretty young girl.

As soon as he sat next to her on the couch, Hasiba gave him the relevant papers for a lawsuit her friend Rihab wanted to take to court. She asked him to read them and give her his opinion as a judge. He quickly examined the papers and told her that the lawsuit was hopeless. She replied to him that she loved her friend Rihab and she wanted to help her in any possible way. He told her that he also loved her friend Rihab and that he also wanted to help her in any possible way because she was an angel that had escaped from heaven and a glance from her could resuscitate the dead. She deserved all the best; but sadly, her lawsuit wouldn't make it in court. The lawsuit could only succeed if some of the information in it were changed.

Hasiba gave Nassouh a blotter and a pen and said to him with a sly smile: "Let's get to work, you know that Rihab and I can offer the best services money can buy."

He asked her about his recompense, and she moved closer to his ears to whisper it to him. He swiftly grabbed his beard with the fingers of his right hand and, while he caressed it, he said to Hasiba: "By God, that is some recompense! A promise is a promise!"

He took the blotter and the pen from her hands and focused on falsifying the lawsuit thoroughly and accurately until he completed it. He proudly gave it to his wife, confident that the lawsuit was unbeatable. She smiled cunningly and advised him to gather his strength and prepare to meet her friend soon.

The Old Dress

On the very night of her marriage to Mahmoud al-Khal, Mu'nis al-'Allam's daughter Leila was kidnapped by an unknown man who returned her after three days, looking worn out as if she had not slept a wink the whole time. Everybody knew of Mahmoud's love for Leila, and he vowed to kill the man who had kidnapped her and drink his blood.

However, the information that Leila provided did not help identify the kidnapper. He remained unidentified, and nobody knew anything about him. Mahmoud married Leila after her family agreed to reduce the amount of her dowry after long negotiations that lasted months and required the opinion of mediators who were able to ascertain the difference in value between a new dress and an old one. His friends envied Mahmoud, for he could enjoy everything he had always dreamt of for less than half the price.

The Epidemic

Dalal was running around in the courtyard, whining about how bored she was. Then, she rushed toward the front door. Her mother shouted, warning her that playing in the street with boys wasn't suitable for a girl like her who was less than seven years old. Dalal ignored the warning, opened the door, and went out.

Her mother bellowed in a threatening tone: "You will regret it when I tell your father about it."

Dalal smiled with contempt and said to her mother: "Dad died, so what could he do?"

Her mother told her in a serious tone: "He will get angry, visit you every night in your sleep, and he will tell you that he doesn't love you."

"You are wrong. My father loves me, and he will love me more and hate you when I tell him what you do every night with our neighbor, the butcher" replied Dalal.

Dalal's mother raised her head, looking up to the sky, and said with an angry tone: "May God never make you grow up."

Her prayers weren't answered. Dalal grew up and became a beautiful girl who was often surrounded by her admirers. Dalal wasn't ashamed or bothered when the police told her, while suppressing their laugh and embarrassment, that Salah Mahshoum, who lived in a house nearby, had filed a complaint against her, claiming that she assaulted him. The police were surprised when she confessed and without denying it. She said that he was boring, always hugging her, kissing her, and clinging to her. So, she rejected him and taught him that a beginning had always an inevitable end. She also said she knew that the law would force her to choose between marrying him and making up for her mistake or going to prison. She didn't like prisons, she was afraid of them and couldn't live there. Therefore, acknowledging her mistake, Dalal married Salah in a ceremony just for family members.

On the first night of her marriage, Dalal couldn't sleep until the muezzin called the dawn prayer. In her sleep, she saw her father was sad, upset, and furious with her. He swore to her that he never loved her. She cried and tears filled her face. She woke up to find her husband, clinging to her and fast asleep like a baby with his lips moving as if he was sucking his mother's breasts. She made sure she didn't move in fear of waking him up and went back to sleep. She saw her father again preparing a massive bonfire. He carried helpless women and threw them into the fire until he got tired. Then, he looked at his daughter with reproach and blame, so she rushed to help him with enthusi-asm and vigor, which made him smile satisfied. He just sat there, watching her, and smoking a cigarette after a cigarette. Dalal got excited when she glimpsed her mother among the women and rushed to her with open arms. As soon as the mother touched her, it was as if the baby girl that Dalal once was had come back. Her mother carried her home and put her in a small bed next to her bed where she lay down. She called one of her men and barked at him, telling him off for being late for the date. Then, Dalal burst out crying, so her mother rushed to calm her down by putting a sheep doll near her head, a little white sheep that bleated her in a faint calm tone making her to fall asleep. Later, the bleating got mixed with the pant-ing of a man and a woman and the squeaking of a bed that was shaking with violent movements. When Dalal woke up hungry and crying the next morning, her mother brought her face to her chest. She put in her mouth a nipple overflowing with milk. She, then, told the man who was putting his clothes on while he was stretching and yawning that she wanted to live until she could see her daughter coveted by men.

Waiting for a Woman

Faris al-Muaz was born headless. His mother cried, the doctor sighed in horror, his father clung to the walln and the nurses ran through the corridors of the hospital.

Contrary to what the doctors had predicted, Faris didn't die and lived a long life. He couldn't see, nor hear or talk. He couldn't complain, nor work. Many people envied him and said that he had actually earned more than he lost.

Faris never stopped waiting for a headless woman to be born, so they could meet and give birth to a new breed of humans, hoping his waiting would not last too long.

The First Gifts

Mu'awiya al-Hanafi dressed as a cop and walked with a smile on his face on the sidewalk of a street overcrowded with people, cars, and bikes. He walked slowly, enjoying the furtive looks of fear people gave him. His smile faded when he noticed two men heaping insults on one another in loud and angry voices. He closely observed the scene with a stern look on his face, upset at the little attention the two men paid to him. One of the two men was tall and fat, whereas the other one had a brown face, was thin, and his hair was short, which made him look as if he just came out of prison. Soon, the profanity they directed at each other became fierce punches and kicks. The fat man was able to hit his opponent harder and more effectively, but the brown-faced man took out a straight razor and ripped the fat man's chest open with a sudden blow. The fat man drew back, gasping, and terrified. He leaned on a wall where a number of death notices had been put up, crying in a pool of blood.

Mu'awiya swiftly grabbed the brown-faced man firmly, stopping him from getting close to his opponent. He suggested that he calm down, be patient, and curb his wrath. He instructed the people who had gathered around to go back to their business and took the brown-faced man to a café nearby. As they sat at one of the tables, Mu'awiya said to the man: "You wouldn't turn down a nice cup of coffee to relax a bit, would you? How do you take it?"

"Strong, with a little sugar," said the brown-faced man.

Mu'awiya got the waiter's attention and ordered two cups of coffee, one strong and bitter and the other sweet and piping hot. He offered the brown-faced man a cigarette and said to him: "Go ahead, smoke and take it easy."

The brown-faced man lit his cigarette and nervously blew the smoke from his mouth and nose.

"Were you fighting because you belong to two opposing political parties?" asked him Mu'awiya.

"We were fighting because he accused me of having an affair with his wife. I confessed and told him that I only see her when he's at work and she's got nothing else to do, so he got jealous, lost his temper, and lunged at me."

"My God, people have really lost their minds," said Mu'awiya in a heavy-hearted voice. "How could he attack you knowing that you're stronger than him? Does his wife deserve this bereavement?"

"Had she only been pretty, I would have been able to forget her easily. Beauty isn't rare among women after all."

He got closer to Mu'awiya's ear and whispered something about the woman that made him gasp as though something had inadvertently obstructed his breathing.

"That's what true women are like: they are like a fire that men try to put out with water, except the water has the effect of airplanes petrol," said the brown-faced man.

The waiter brought the two cups of coffee and the brown-faced man tried to pay for them. However, Mu'awiya stopped him and paid the bill. He reproached him for forgetting that he was a guest and guests are to be treated with honor. The brown-faced man downed a big gulp of his coffee and licked his lips in appreciation. "I have a request but I don't know how to put it," said Mu'awiya with a voice that made the brown-faced man reach for his blood-soaked razor. "You can ask me anything, don't be ashamed," said the brown-faced man.

"Would you sell me your razor?" said Mu'awiya.

"How am I supposed to shave my beard every morning then?" said the brown-faced man in astonishment.

"Buy another one," Mu'awiya said.

"Why don't you buy a new one?" said the brown-faced man.

Mu'awiya snorted in disapproval and said that a brand-new razor is like a pretty and cold woman. The brown-faced man laughed, took the razor out of his pocket, and gave it to Mu'awiya, saying it was a gift and that he didn't have to pay for it. Mu'awiya insisted that he should pay, but the brown-faced man reiterated his position and patted Mu'awiya on his shoulder with genuine admiration while saying: "You deserve the finest gifts, I wish all cops were like you."

Mu'awiya smiled and blushed in a state of un-easiness. He shoved the blood-dripping razor in his pocket and mumbled something to express his grat-itude. Once more, before leaving, he reminded the brown-faced man to stay calm, be patient, and to al-ways control his rage. He left the café and went back to a street packed with people, cars, and bikes. He walked slowly, trying to figure out what clothes he would wear the following day.

The One with the Fez

Mansour al-Haaf was a man from Damascus, feared and revered by the fiercest men. A man with the composure of a calm sea, imperturbable and self-possessed. Unlike his dagger, which was hot-tempered and stabbed its opponents despicably without killing them. Its sharp blade ripped apart their flesh and nothing, not even a last minute apology, could save them from it. He would gladly go to jail as though he was going to a summer resort, and when he was discharged, he would say: "Only a stupid man would be happy to move from a small jail to a bigger one."

Mansour al-Haaf loved his wife Naziha since the first moment he laid eyes on her, although he never openly expressed his ardor to her. He would not feel ashamed to publicly acknowledge that his wife's orders were to be obeyed without hesitation, to the extent that if she had asked him to shave off his moustache, he would have done so immediately. However, his attitude changed when Naziha suggested that he should take off his fez. He became a distant and rude man. He frowned and proudly claimed that the fez was the man's embellishment. She said the fez was an ugly, obnoxious guest. He said he was born wearing it and he would die like that. She said she couldn't bear the sight of a fez. He said fez were for men, head-scarves for women and branches for trees.

One day, his wife said to him impatiently in an angry voice: "Either you divorce your fez or you divorce me!" Mansour al-Haaf was furious, but he didn't draw his dagger. He said to her: "Our house's door is wide enough for a camel to walk through it. Go, run to your family. You're divorced . . . You're divorced . . . You're divorced."

Naziha left the house in shock, bareheaded, crying in a desperate voice: "Help!"

A nosy, curious wind carried her lamentation to the ears of the French general Henri Gouraud, who set off to save her and led his troops victoriously into Damascus, stained with the blood of the city's sons killed in the battle against the French at Maysalun in 1920. Damascus received him with the desolation of a falcon trapped in a cage, deprived of its sky. However, a clique of dignitaries and their servants rushed to carry General Gouraud's car on their backs to express their warm reception to him. His hand, covered by leather gloves, shook those of the dignitaries who were so honored they were shaking.

General Gouraud rushed to visit Saladin's tomb and said to him in satisfaction: "Lo, we're back!" Saladin, giving voice to a land whose tears had been washed away by a sudden rain and who was just regaining its strength after losing it for many years, replied to General Gouraud, saying: "And yet one day you will return to your country inside black coffins."

General Gouraud didn't pay attention to what was being said to him and proceeded to stroll around the city of Damascus with a happy face, surrounded by his many guards carrying modern weapons, prepared to shoot even a cloud had it dared to cross the sky unauthorized. He walked the city alleys slowly, like someone who wished to spend the rest of their life in that place, but he grumbled at the sight of those red hats on the men's heads. He returned to his office and issued a strict and menacing ban on the fez and its production. All the fezzes were thrown into the Barada River and men had to walk with their heads uncovered, staggering as though they were barefooted. But Mansour al-Haaf's head clung resolutely to the fez, so the French soldiers captured him and threw him in jail without interrogation or trial.

When General Gouraud became bored of seducing women, eating fat food, and drinking wine, and was keen of trying a different kind of amusement, he summoned the one man who had disobeyed his order and kept his fez. In shackles, Mansour al-Haaf was taken into a spacious hall full of army officers and soldiers. He stood in front of the general, who asked him in an irritated tone: "Are you aware of the punishment that awaits those who dare to disobey my orders?"

Mansour al-Haaf smiled and answered calmly, "Nothing more than death."

"I advise you to avoid playing the brave and fearless because that won't do you any good."

Mansour al-Haaf tried to speak, but he stammered as he pictured in his mind the planet Earth in the form of a big fez inside which the cold bodies of dead soldiers from different nationalities were falling. He heard General Gouraud asking him sarcastically: "What's with you? Have you become mute?"

"To die for the fez is an honor every man wishes for," replied Mansour al-Haaf confidently.

"I like your fez," said General Gouraud whilst examining it, pretending never to have seen one before. "It would make a nice exotic gift for my wife. How much would you sell it for? I will give you ten liras in gold . . . twenty . . . a hundred . . . a thousand . . . two thousand."

Mansour al-Haaf interrupted him: "My fez isn't for sale. I wouldn't sell it even for all the wealth of Harun and Qarun."

General Gouraud became furious and, pointing to Mansour, barked to his soldiers: "Execute him immediately!"

"A dead animal's corpse doesn't contaminate the sea."

One of the officers approached General Gouraud and asked him in a low voice: "How should we execute him though? By hanging or by firing squad?"

"Listen," said General Gouraud, addressing his deputies, sounding like a school teacher talking to his young pupils. "Every country has its heritage and, as the bearers of civilization, it is our duty to respect it. We are now in a country whose population usually employs decapitation."

General Gouraud's soldiers rushed to make Mansour al-Haaf kneel and bow down, but he shouted in disapproval: "This is unfair. Why can I not be asked about my last wish?"

"Ask him," said General Gouraud to the soldiers. "He may want to do ablutions."

"What is your last wish?" asked the soldier.

"I want to be executed at my ex-wife's feet," said Mansour.

"Where would you like to be buried?" the soldier asked him.

"My flesh doesn't discriminate what sort of worms eat it."

"Do you know what you're dying for?" asked him General Gouraud.

Mansour al-Haaf's face went pale, but his voice remained calm and confident when he said: "All things are ephemeral but his face . . ."

"Whose face?" said General Gouraud. "Who are you referring to?"

"Say: I seek refuge in the Lord of mankind, the king of mankind, the God of mankind, from the sneaking whisperer, so do not weaken and do not grieve, and you will be superior, and we destroyed completely all the great works and buildings which Pharaoh and his people erected."

"Are you blind?" said to him General Gouraud. "We are superior, we have destroyed our enemies."

"Our Lord! Bestow on us mercy from thyself and dispose of our affair for us in the right way . . . the Approaching Day has approached, of it there is no remover but God."

In that moment, bent down on his knees as he was, Mansour al-Haaf appeared to General Gouraud like a confused, obnoxious, presumptuous, repulsive, stupid human being. To General Gouraud, Mansour didn't realize what was happening to him and engaged in a duel, happy to face a tragic ending, persuaded that he was unbeaten, reciting someone else's words like a broken record. General Gouraud tried to contain his fury, shouting to his soldiers: "Execute him now!"

The sword fell on Mansour al-Haaf's neck, chopping off his head and making it roll over like a ball kicked about by a child. The fez, though, remained stuck to Mansour's head and General Gouraud instructed his men to pull it off but, no matter how hard they tried, they couldn't succeed. That fez was like an irremovable part of the head. General Gouraud ordered to burn that head and its fez. The soldiers proceeded to prepare a fire so big that it could burn an entire cow. When the fire went out, the head, which had once been full of caprice and stood high proudly between the shoulders, had turned into ashes. But the fez remained red and intact, as though nothing had touched it.

Upon finding out what had happened, General Gouraud was baffled, irritated, and disoriented. He ordered that the fez be sent to France's scientific laboratories to be analyzed and discover the conundrum of its occult strength. However, the fez disappeared in mysterious circumstances and didn't get to visit France. It was seen one day on the head of a brown-colored man firing shots from his revolver toward a warplane flying over Damascus, bombing one of its quarters.

It was seen again one day on the head of a man who made coffins and stashed them for a time when their prices would double and they would be sold in the black market. And it was seen again a third time. It had become a happy red ball kicked about by laughing children.

The First Reduction

Abd al-Nabi al-Sabban was a big, tall man with broad shoulders. He was arrested and accused of breathing too much air, more than he was entitled to. He didn't deny the accusation and said that it was due to the size of his lungs. He was then transferred to a hospital, which he left after several weeks as a new man. He was now short with narrow shoulders and with two tiny lungs, and he consumed a daily amount of air smaller than what was officially allowed to him.

The Green Bird

Abu Hayyan al-Tawhidi burned everything he had written on paper and looked at its ashes with satisfaction, letting out a sigh of relief. He felt hungry but he didn't find anything to eat in his house. He wiped his mouth with the back of his hand and thanked God. He stood in front of a mirror, but he didn't like what he saw. He metamorphosed into a lamb, then into a cat, then into a wolf, and eventually into a green-feathered bird. He left through the window, flew over the houses, and landed on a tree branch. He looked eagerly at a man sitting in his palace's garden surrounded by his many cronies, servants, and bodyguards. The man was contemplating everything around him and found it beautiful. The grass was green, the trees were green, and their branches were overloaded with ripe fruit. The sky was blue, the sun was shining, and flowers were colorful and sundry. "Is there anyone in the world happier than me?" wondered the man in a loud, ecstatic voice.

People around him vied to reassure him that he was indeed the happiest, strongest, richest, most compassionate and generous man. This irritated the green bird, which metamorphosed into a black crow. Its caws, in turn, irritated the man, who ordered his bodyguards to oust the bird from his garden. They tried but failed and bowed their heads in shame while the crow persisted cawing and flying from one tree to another. Eventually the man was forced to leave the garden, which brought joy to the bird who flew away until it reached an alley and landed on an overhead power line. The crow observed a group of loud, cheerful kids as they were playing and, as its rancor faded, it turned into a chirping sparrow. The kids didn't notice it and carried on playing and laughing. The sparrow flew away again and saw a fierce battle taking place between two armies. The sparrow turned into a warplane, dropped its bombs onto the two armies and wiped them out. The plane flew away from those torn corpses and hovered over a prison yard where the guards were beating the inmates with hard sticks. The plane razed the prison, and the inmates promptly set out to build a new one with taller walls. The plane saw a ship crossing the sea, whose passengers thought that the deluge would smite the whole earth. The plane turned into a white dove which flew and returned to the ship shortly after, holding in its beak a green branch dripping blood or perhaps red ink.

The Wizard

The hands of a five-year-old boy were tied behind his back, his eyes blindfolded under a dark cloth. Five soldiers were standing in front of him, ready to fire their guns and execute their officer's orders. Their officer raised his commanding voice and they quickly pointed their rifles at the child's heart. The officer ordered them to shoot, but his stern voice got mixed up with the child's laugh in the soldiers' ears, which reminded the first soldier of his pretty wife laughing. The second soldier recalled his bed near a window overlooking a river. The third remembered a street abounding with trees where he used to walk and chat with a friend. The fourth remembered the day his father taught him to fish on the seaside when he was a child. The fifth recalled the way his mother got older suddenly on the day she fell ill.

The five soldiers obeyed the military order and fired their rifles at the officer, knocking him to the ground with five bloody holes in his chest. They waited with no regrets for somebody to shoot them, but they remained alive, unlike the commanders who ordered the shooting.

An Empty Grave

The general was a man with lungs, a stomach, a large intestine and a small intestine, a liver, and arteries filled with red blood. There was nothing peculiar about him except that he was the general of an army at war in a foreign country. He found his job boring and devoid of excitement. He dreamed of working on a farm breeding cows and goats one day, or maybe in a hospital for the disabled and elderly. The general was a stern and unhappy man. He would only find delight when he pictured a little bird trying to fly unsuccessfully; or when he imagined his dutiful soldiers occupying villages and cities, eagerly destroying all the houses and killing their inhabitants; or when he dreamed of equipping his soldiers with weapons capable of exterminating hundreds of thousands of people in a few seconds, but avoided using them so they could still kill their enemies slowly and with greater pleasure.

One day, he felt a different kind of delight as he noticed that new black hair had begun to sprout on his head replacing the little grey hair. This made him proud because it was an indication of his masculinity and of the return of youth. The hair on his whole body grew increasingly, covering his skin with a thick, heavy layer, and his facial features changed gradually. As he couldn't sleep one night, he felt a mysterious force traverse his whole body. He jumped out of the bed, stretched in front of the mirror, looking at himself thoroughly and saw that he had metamorphosed into a dreadful hyena, covered in a thick fur. His fingers became claws, his teeth turned into cuspids, and he reveled in his transmutation. He was starving, irresistibly, so hungry that he jumped on his sleeping wife's neck, and killed her before she could wake up. He didn't like her flaccid flesh, though, and left her disgusted. He pounced on her baby son, who had been sleeping with a smile on his face, and he was impressed with his tender and juicy meat. One of the general's guards was standing at attention outside the bedroom, with his finger on the trigger of his gun, prepared to deal with any sudden danger. He was shocked at the sight of a hyena coming out of the room dripping with blood, so he shot it and killed it. The rest of the guards arrived, rushing and screaming in agitation, and they found the remains of the wife and her son. They did not find the general, though, and it was widely believed that the hyena ate his entire body without leaving anything to bury.

The Black Wings

When he was a child, Umar Yasser was always laughing for no reason, but as an adult, he loathed laughter and never laughed again. One morning, he found himself an old man lying on his bed. He closed his eyes and ignored his wife who kept reminding him to go to work. Suddenly, a gruff cop with two black wings came out of the wardrobe and said to Umar in a harsh commanding tone: "Come on, get up! You will be late for work."

Umar Yasser replied: "I have worked for fifty years for nothing, so I'm not working today, nor tomorrow, nor any other day."

The cop said, "But if other people work and you don't, the factories' output will drop."

Umar Yasser asked him, "Are you a policeman or an agent working for the factory owners?"

"If you do not work, you will starve," said the cop.

"I will eat dirt and wood, and if I crave meat, I will eat my old wife," replied Umar.

The cop warned and threatened him: "If you do not work, you will have lost your reason to carry on living and you will have sentenced yourself to an early death."

Umar Yasser laughed and told the black-winged policeman: "Whoever clings to this life is a stupid fool son of a bitch."

Umar Yasser closed his eyes persistently. He lay on his bed and surrendered to the cop's fingers strangling him. When his wife saw him lying motionless, she stared at him amazed and said to him in a mix of grief and joy: "Alhamdulillah cousin, you laughed before you died, I wish I knew why you were laughing, so I could laugh too."

Umar Yasser tried to fulfil her request, but she could not understand what he was mumbling. As his body was being lowered into his final resting place, those who had gathered there were saddened, everyone except his loving wife. She was secretly smiling and was gripped by a mysterious wily joy.

The River

Jabir Al-Mallahi loved a woman who didn't care for him, she thought little of him, and she was happily married to a young husband that many men scrambled for. Jabir was filled with sorrow, bitterness, and shame. He decided to abandon his house in resentment and only came back after spending ten years in remote cities. His neighbors came to visit and congratulate him. They asked him to tell them what he had seen in those extraordinary cities where he had lived. Jabir was confused, he told them that he was tired and that he would tell them another time.

Weeks later, he pretended not to have heard what they had asked, and he talked about something else. Months later, he said that he had forgotten what he saw and what he remembered wasn't worth mentioning. Years later, he denied that he had ever traveled or lived far from his neighborhood. His neighbors believed him as they would often imagine things that didn't exist and events that never took place. They had only imagined that Jabir Al-Mallahi left his neighborhood and was away for ten years.

Jabir Al-Mallahi suddenly got married to a woman whom he fell in love with, but only after they had tied the knot. However, when he decided that he wanted to have children, he found out that she was sterile. However, he didn't divorce her, nor did he marry another woman. He lived in a house with a garden and three fruit trees. He spent most of his time looking after the trees and refused to harvest its fruit. He was content with just observing as the trees blossomed, bore fruit, and ripened, and then withered, dried out, rotted, and fell to the ground. He and his wife were dispirited in autumn and winter, but they would rejoice in spring and summer.

One morning, they were surprised that all tree fruits had been stolen. The branches had been spitefully broken as if the anonymous thieves were taking revenge on the trees for destroying their homes. Jabir and his wife were devastated as if they had lost their own children. Jabir sold his house and resumed his journey to remote cities with his sterile wife.

The End of a Long Wait

The day Marwan al-'Ulabi died his three sons gathered around his cold body with their chins upon their chests. They shed copious tears, which their hands did not try to wipe, busy as they were dividing everything their father owned.

The eldest took his underwear and his shoes; the second took his shirt, his trousers, and his socks; the youngest son took his coat. Marwan al-'Ulabi closed his eyes, ashamed of his nudity, then in a feeble, shaking voice, he asked his sons: "Which one of you is going to inherit my debts?" They looked at each other in astonishment and agreed that what they heard was nothing but a hallucination, because a corpse cannot speak.

The Pursuit

Bahija yawned, annoyed while her husband Hamid was absorbed reading a magazine. She tried to lure him to talk to her, but he begged her to let him finish an article about a famous dancer who had become rich and was thinking of quitting her profession. Bahija said to him with a frown on her face: "What if I also dance a year or two and then retire?"

Hamid sulked and was about to retort when wailings rose from a place nearby. The magazine slipped through his fingers, and he stood up with a yellowish face. His voice quivered as he kept saying: "oh my God . . ."

Bahija laughed and told him as she was leaving the room: "Don't worry. This is our neighbor wailing, rejoicing at her husband's success in the primary school examinations."

Bahija returned shortly to hand Hamid a cup, saying to him: "Come on, drink up your coffee or you will be late for your doctor's appointment."

Hamid asked her: "Where is the coffee? This is milk, not coffee."

"This is coffee," replied Bahija.

"Coffee is black and milk is white," retorted Hamid.

Bahija said to him: "You speak as if you were still sleeping. Coffee is white and milk is black."

In a hasty move, Hamid put the cup on the coffee table, sprang up from the couch and approached the open window. He saw white bulls flying without wings in a clear red sky.

"Come quickly and see," shouted Hamid to Bahija incredulous.

Bahija clung to his back and asked him in a cunning, low voice: "Can I show you something that is in this room which is nicer and cuter than these silly birds, and although you could see it, you don't pay attention to it?"

Hamid heard a rough cough coming from another room. Astonished, he looked at Bahija wondering, and she explained: "This is my new friend Jalal, he arrived late last night. I felt pity for him and I put him up here."

Hamid said to himself: "I must be asleep, everything I see and hear must be a dream."

Hamid closed his eyes and opened them only when their neighbor let out a zaghruta to celebrate her lazy son's success in the baccalaureate exams. The strange man vanished from the house, birds were flying in the sky, and Bahija gave him his bitter black coffee, which he drank hastily before heading over to the doctor's clinic. He was walking on a broad street when he saw women gathered together to murder their children while lulling them to sleep with songs full of tenderness; young men with taut muscles slaughtering their fathers with big rusty knives; men beating their wives despite their shrieking and soldiers snatching babies from their mother's breasts, knocking them to the ground and raping the mothers as if they wanted to kill them.

Hamid clung to a wall and wished to fade away. He closed his eyes and only tried to open them when a soldier blindfolded him with a black cloth and ordered him not to move. Hamid heard the sound of bullets firing and fell to the ground with two bullet holes, one on his forehead and another one in his heart. He ran home horrified and told Bahija with a quavering voice that he had been shot and he was dead. She was annoyed because he had left burns on his new expensive suit, torn it and stained it with his black blood. Hamid swallowed his irritation and told Bahija in a quiet tone that his blood was red, not black. She told him that even as a dead man his ego would still get the best of him. She reproached him for missing his doctor's appointment and advised him to endure his health problems silently and without complaining. He didn't utter a word and ran back to the street to find it covered in corpses.

His body got stuck with the other corpses, over-whelmed by a sense of comfort he had never felt be-fore, indifferent to the stern cries ordering the second execution.

Her Fourth Promise

Hamdan and Rima first met at a political rally and Hamdan fell in love with her at first sight. After a while, he accused her of being heartless, so she promised she would love him when a man went to the moon. A man did go to moon and even walked around there. Rima didn't break her promise and she did love him. Then he pestered her, asking her to marry him, and she promised she would marry him when the Soviet Union became capitalist. When the Soviet Union turned to capitalism, Rima kept her promise, and married him. He considered himself the happiest man in the world. However, a few months later, she caught him sobbing gloomily. He said that a house without children was desolate and unbearable. She promised that she would give birth to a boy when the Berlin Wall fell, and when it did fall and its stones were sold to aficionados of archaeology, Rima honored her promise to Hamdan and had a boy who was the spitting image of his father except for the moustache. Hamdan only rejoiced for a few days. Then, he started to complain to Rima about his empty pockets, the widespread unemployment, and meagre salaries. She promised him that his conditions were going to improve when America became communist. America did become a communist country, with red flags fluttering in its skies, but Hamdan's situation didn't change. His pockets remained empty, unemployment was still widespread, and salaries didn't improve.

Dear Beloved Homeland

There was once a tree that was strong and had many branches. It stood tirelessly day and night in the back garden of a house. Season after season, the tree became stronger and stronger, its trunk thickened and its branches grew, rising high above and expanding in all directions. One of the branches extended unexpectedly to come very close to a large window and the other branches envied it because it could see what the others couldn't.

The branch saw what was going on inside the room. It sighed in astonishment, frightened, upset, sad, disgusted, or whining like a dying patient, yet it refused to talk to the other branches about what it could see on the pretext that it was busy following what was going on inside the room and had no time to chat.

One day, when it tried to tell the other branches what it had seen, it couldn't speak. Suddenly, the other branches realized that they were all young and fresh, covered with green leaves, unlike that dry and frail branch whose leaves were wilting early, which stopped observing what went on inside the house until one windy night, it fell off the tree. From that moment on, none of the branches attempted to approach the house's windows.

The Last Story

The patrons of the café accused the local hakawati—a white-haired man with wrinkles running through his face and a thick moustache—of telling old, tired, unbearably boring stories. They asked him to tell entertaining stories, but the hakawati didn't utter a word. He was content with a conceited silence and smiled mockingly. As the patrons' roars dwindled, the hakawati spoke confidently. He promised to tell them a strange tale that had never been told before and that would make them sleep in such a way as if they were still embryos in their mothers' wombs.

Silence took over the café, the patrons looked eagerly at the hakawati, who in turn smiled derisively and started telling a new story. The patrons fell asleep, and so did the brother who was interested in killing his own brother, all inhabitants of planet Earth, and so did the hakawati himself. Grass grew on the road's tar; birds built their nests on top of cars; doves lay down their eggs on the dusty wings of airplanes, and deer, elephants, and tigers wandered the streets lazily.

Glossary

Abaya ('abā'a): a long cloak, usually black, typically worn with a veil.

Antara ibn Shaddad (525–608 CE), also known as Antar: pre-Islamic poet, later the subject of a popular cycle of traditional heroic legends.

Farid Al-Atrash (1916–74): popular Egyptian composer, singer, and actor.

Gouraud, Henri (1867–1946): French general, Commissioner of the Levant (1919–22), famous for having defeated the Syrian resistance in the Battle of Maysaloun in 1920. In its aftermath, France took control of the territory that came to be known as the French Mandate for Syria and Lebanon, which lasted until 1946 when Syria and Lebanon obtained their independence.

Hakawati: a storyteller, a man who tells or reads out stories in a local café, typically at night during the month of Ramadan.

Zaghruta: a wavering, high-pitched, vocal sound heard at celebrations, also translated "trilling" or "ululation."

Zakaria Tamer is a Syrian writer. He is the author of numerous short story collections, including *Breaking Knees: Modern Arabic Short Stories from Syria* and *Tigers on the Tenth Day*.

Alessandro Columbu is a lecturer in Arabic at the University of Westminster in London. He is the author of *Zakariyya Tamir and the Politics of the Syrian Short Story*.

Mireia Costa Capallera is a professional translator. She has a masters degree in Contemporary Arabic Studies and speaks six languages.

Nader K. Uthman (PhD, Columbia) is Senior Preceptor in Arabic and Director of the Modern Language Programs in the Department of Near Eastern Languages and Civilizations at Harvard University. He is the author of *Traces*, the English translation of Gamal al-Ghitani's *Nithar Al-Mahw* (American University of Cairo Press, 2020).

Printed in the USA
CPSIA information can be obtained
at www.ICGtesting.com
LVHW091225151223
7664892LV00004B/419